O9-AID-046

"That depends on what you want out of this."

"Your help," she said. "I want you to help me to save my home."

"That's it?"

Pressing her lips together, she nodded.

"At any price?"

"Almost any price," she modified, with a nervous touch of her tongue to her suddenly dry upper lip.

"Okay." He nodded. "Then let us see if we can find the ceiling on your *almost* any price. But on my terms, *querida.* And nonnegotiable terms at that."

The *almost* test. She could hear it coming. "What kind of terms?" she asked huskily.

"I need a wife," he announced. "And I need one quickly. You, *meu querida,* are in the fortunate position of suiting my requirements."

Three popular Harlequin Presents® authors
bring you an exciting new miniseries:

*Three half brothers, scattered to opposite sides
of the globe: each must find a bride
in order to find each other.*

Book 1: *The Ramirez Bride*
by Emma Darcy
September 2005 #2487

Book 2: *The Brazilian's Blackmailed Bride*
by Michelle Reid
October 2005 #2499

Anton Luis Scott-Lee has to marry the woman
who so callously rejected him years ago. Cristina
has no choice but to accept Luis's demand for
marriage, but Luis will find that his new bride
can't or won't fulfill all of her wedding vows....

Look out for the next title in this trilogy—
coming soon!

Book 3: *The Disobedient Virgin*
by Sandra Marton
November 2005

Available only from Harlequin Presents®!

Michelle Reid

THE BRAZILIAN'S BLACKMAILED BRIDE

The Ramirez Brides

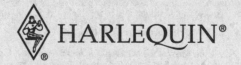

HARLEQUIN®

TORONTO • NEW YORK • LONDON
AMSTERDAM • PARIS • SYDNEY • HAMBURG
STOCKHOLM • ATHENS • TOKYO • MILAN • MADRID
PRAGUE • WARSAW • BUDAPEST • AUCKLAND

If you purchased this book without a cover you should be aware
that this book is stolen property. It was reported as "unsold and
destroyed" to the publisher, and neither the author nor the
publisher has received any payment for this "stripped book."

ISBN 0-373-12493-7

THE BRAZILIAN'S BLACKMAILED BRIDE

First North American Publication 2005.

Copyright © 2005 by Michelle Reid.

All rights reserved. Except for use in any review, the reproduction or
utilization of this work in whole or in part in any form by any electronic,
mechanical or other means, now known or hereafter invented, including
xerography, photocopying and recording, or in any information storage
or retrieval system, is forbidden without the written permission of the
publisher, Harlequin Enterprises Limited, 225 Duncan Mill Road,
Don Mills, Ontario, Canada M3B 3K9.

All characters in this book have no existence outside the imagination of
the author and have no relation whatsoever to anyone bearing the same
name or names. They are not even distantly inspired by any individual
known or unknown to the author, and all incidents are pure invention.

This edition published by arrangement with Harlequin Books S.A.

® and TM are trademarks of the publisher. Trademarks indicated with
® are registered in the United States Patent and Trademark Office, the
Canadian Trade Marks Office and in other countries.

www.eHarlequin.com

Printed in U.S.A.

CHAPTER ONE

THERE was an old-world elegance about the walnut-panelled room that somehow scorned the idea that anyone would be tasteless enough to raise their voice in anger in here. Under normal circumstances Anton Luis Ferreira Scott-Lee certainly would not have dreamt of doing it.

But there was nothing normal about this situation, and the anger was certainly here, pulsing away in the background, even if it was safely encased in ice right now.

'I will have to resign,' he announced, effectively throwing the two people in the room with him into a frozen state of horror and dismay.

His mother was too young, at fifty, and much too beautiful to be a widow—but apparently *not* too young, after marrying at the youthful age of nineteen, to have clocked up a murky past which had now come back to haunt her.

'But—*meu querido*...' She recovered first to speak shakily. 'You cannot possibly resign!'

'I don't think that I have a damn choice.'

Maria Ferreira Scott-Lee flinched, her liquid brown eyes wrenching down and away from her son's hard expression.

'Don't be crazy, boy,' Maximilian Scott-Lee thrust out impatiently. 'This has nothing to do with the bank! Let's try to keep some perspective here.'

Max wanted perspective? Switching his gaze from his mother to the man he had lovingly called Uncle for all of his life, Anton felt a sudden rushing urge to smash a fist into his beloved face!

No perspective there, he thought as he swung away to

5

aim his bitter black mood at the view beyond one of the long casement windows that lined the beautifully appointed study of this, the Scott-Lees' Belgravia home.

It was a lousy day out there. The rain, lashing down from an iron-grey sky, was battering what leaves were left clinging to the trees down onto the square below. Anton knew how those leaves felt. Two hours ago a bright, calm winter day had been shining on London and he had been attending a board meeting, supremely confident in his place as chairman of the old and prestigious Scott-Lee Bank.

Now look at him, cast adrift like those storm-battered leaves out there.

A muscle flicked at his clenched jaw, emphasising the stubborn cleft in the centre of his chin...a cleft he had not thought to question until today, just as he had not thought of questioning many things about himself that were now staring him hard in the face.

And why should he have? Born the adored only child of Brazilian beauty Maria Ferreira and wealthy English banker Sebastian Scott-Lee...or so he'd believed until today...he'd naturally taken it for granted that he'd inherited his lean dark Latin looks from his Brazilian mother and his shrewd business mind from his late and still deeply missed English father.

At first, when he had read the letter from a Brazilian called Enrique Ramirez who was claiming to be his real father, he'd thought it was some kind of sick joke. It had taken this confrontation with his mother and his uncle to have his joke theory crushed right out of him. Now he was having to come to terms with the ugly fact that not only was this Ramirez guy telling the truth, but the man he'd always believed to be his real father had known about his mother's affair with Enrique and that Anton was not his real son! A very hush-hush adoption had secured his legal place in Sebastian Scott-Lee's life, along with the abiding wish that Anton should never find out the truth.

'You know as well as I do that without you the bank will collapse,' Max pushed into the thickened silence. 'You *are* the bank, Anton. If you resign people will want to know why you've gone. The truth will inevitably come out, because juicy stuff like this always does, and the family name will be—'

'This truth didn't come out,' Anton said harshly.

'Because my brother was careful to make sure that it didn't,' the older man said. 'Who the hell expected Ramirez to come along with his kiss-and-tell last will and testament?'

Kiss and tell, Anton echoed silently, hot, spitting bitterness rolling around inside him and spinning him about.

'Did it never occur to you that *I* had a right to know?' he fired directly at his mother.

Maria tensed, slender fingers mangling the handkerchief she held on her lap. 'Your father did not want—'

'Enrique *bloody* Ramirez is my father!' Anton thundered with explosive force.

The words bounced around the room like the aftershock from an earthquake.

'No.' Maria quivered as she shook her head. 'Enrique w-was a terrible mistake in *my* life, Anton! You did not need—'

'—to know that I've been living a lie for all of my thirty-one years?'

Maria subsided, lifting the handkerchief up to cover her trembling mouth. 'I'm sorry,' she whispered.

'Hearing you say that does not particularly help.'

'You do not understand…'

'You can say that again,' he uttered. 'I thought I was the son of a man I loved and revered above all men. Now I find out I'm the result of an extra-marital affair you enjoyed with some globe-trotting Brazilian polo-playing stud!'

'It wasn't like that.' Maria was going paler by the second. 'I was…with Enrique before I married your f-father.'

'So let me get this right,' Anton said, seeing the red mist of his growing fury swim up across his eyes. 'You had an affair with this guy. He left you pregnant, so you looked around for a gullible substitute to take his place, found Sebastian, and simply foisted me on to him? Is that it?'

'No!' For the first time since this had begun his fine-boned slender mother showed some of her Brazilian fire by shooting to her feet. 'You will not speak to me in this insulting tone, Anton! Your father knew. He *always* knew! I was *honest* with him from the start! He forgave me—and he loved *you* as his own son! *His* name is on your birth certificate. *He* raised you! He was proud of your every achievement and not once did he treat you as anything but the shining light in his life! So don't you *dare* hurt his memory now by turning it into a thing to speak of with contempt!'

Anton flung himself back to the window, seething inside with an eruption of feeling that was crucifying him with anger and bitterness and now tinged with a remorse that placed a sting in his eyes. He'd loved his father, looked up to him in every way a loving son could. When Sebastian had been killed in a freak road accident, Anton had lived for months in a black hole filled with inconsolable grief.

'I always knew I looked nothing like him.' The words arrived hoarse and uneven, pulsing with a deeply felt emotion that forced poor Maria to muffle a sob.

'My brother knew he could not have children, Anton,' Max filtered in huskily. 'He was already aware of that when he met and fell in love with Maria. When she told him about you he saw your coming birth as a gift.'

'A gift he insisted must be kept secret.'

'Don't deny him the right to some pride,' his uncle sighed.

But Anton couldn't think of anyone else's pride right now. 'I'm the son of a Brazilian,' he muttered. 'That makes me about as un-English as I can get. I live like an Englishman, I speak, think, *behave* like an Englishman and—*hell*!' A second explosion of emotion sent his clenched fist pounding into the window's wood casement, because he'd just remembered something. Something he'd spent the last six years trying to forget!

Now a face swam up in front of him—an excruciatingly lovely face, with dark eyes and a lush red mouth. *'But I cannot marry you, Luis, My father will not allow it. Our Portuguese blood must remain pure...'*

'Is Ramirez a Portuguese name?' he demanded roughly.

Still quaking from her son's sudden burst of violence, his mother breathed out a quavering, 'Yes.'

Anton tried for some air but didn't make it. That burst of blistering rage was now pooling inside his head as he replayed once again that unforgettable moment when five feet four inches of Latin scorn had told him that he wasn't good enough for her.

His teeth came together, accentuating that cleft in his chin. Not good enough—*not good enough!* No one before or since had ever dared say such a thing to him.

And he was damned if he was going to give her the chance to say it to him again.

It was then that the ice took over—an ice that those who knew him recognised with dread. Turning to face the room, he saw his mother was trying to fight back the tears still. His uncle just looked old. Maximilian's health wasn't good. He'd suffered his first heart attack which had forced him to retire from the bank, only weeks after his brother's death.

His words to his then grief stricken and shock-battered nephew had been, 'Take the reins, boy. I have every confidence in you to make this family proud.'

That word again—proud.

The muscles around his heart contracted. To be really proud of someone you had to accept them as they were, warts and skeletons alike. These people who claimed to love him only loved a lie they'd constructed to protect their own pride.

Anton stepped back to the desk that had been Sebastian's before he had died leaving everything he possessed—including this house in Belgravia, the family estate near Ascot and the major share in the Scott-Lee Bank—to the person he had been *proud* to call his son.

Well, Anton didn't feel proud of them right now. He felt angry and cheated in too many ways to count.

On the desk lay the documents that had been delivered to him from the lawyer attending to the Ramirez estate. Splintering emotions threatening to take him over again, he sent long blunt ended fingers flicking through the papers until he found the one he was searching for.

'There is more to this,' he clipped out, and saw from beneath his lowered eyelashes his mother and his uncle tense up. 'I am not the only poor swine Ramirez is laying claim to. There are two more like me out there somewhere. Two more sons…'

Two half-brothers with their own lying mothers? His top lip curled in contempt.

'Considering the globe-trotting lifestyle Ramirez enjoyed, they could be anywhere…'

'You mean he does not say?'

'No, not exactly,' Anton drawled cynically. 'How much amusing mileage would he get from making it as simple as that?'

He was already getting to know Ramirez, he noted, and didn't like it—hated it, in fact.

'But he's dead—'

'Yes,' he nodded. 'But still thoroughly enjoying himself at my and my half-brothers' expense.' He heaved in a taut breath. 'You see, he's been keeping tabs on all three of us for years.'

It was like being invaded—spied upon by some faceless stalker. Ramirez knew things about Anton that made the hairs on the back of his neck stand on end. What schools he'd attended, his academic success. He knew about every damn trophy he'd won on the sports field, every major deal in business he'd pulled off. He even knew about all those other trophies he'd notched up in that other sporting arena—his bed.

'He sees us as three sex-obsessed chips off the old block,' he summed up with a white-toothed razor slice. 'So, in his wisdom, he means to teach my brothers and me a lesson in life that apparently he did not grasp until he was too old and it was too late to change what he was.'

He saw his mother wince at the intimacy already honing his tone when he referred to his brothers. Odd. A nerve flicked in his jaw. But he *felt* that intimacy in some deep place inside him, like a newly formed artery feeding the blood link, and it was hungry for more.

'Ramirez was loaded,' he continued. 'And we are not talking about a few paltry million here. He owned diamond mines, emerald mines, some of the richest oil fields in Brazil...' The fact that he could see from their lowered expressions he was telling them things they already knew did not make him feel any better about this. 'We—his three sons—get to share the booty,' he explained with sarcastic bite. 'So long as we fulfil several conditions our dear departed sleazy coward of a father has set out in his will.'

'Enrique was not sleazy,' his mother protested.

'What was he, then?' Anton asked.

'N-nice, h-handsome—like you—charming…'

His mother was still fond of the bastard! Another explosion began to gather.

Maximilian shifted in his seat. 'What kind of conditions?' he questioned.

Anton fought the explosion back down again.

'I can only speak for myself, because that's all that's referred to here,' he said. Then a strange kind of smile hit his mouth. 'I am to mend my philandering ways,' he enlightened. 'Get responsible, find a wife, settle down, produce legitimate progeny—'

'Good God!' Max expelled. 'The man's brain must have been addled by the time he popped it!'

Coming from a confirmed bachelor, his uncle's attitude made sense.

'It makes me wonder what my brothers need to do before they win the right to meet me.'

'You don't need to do anything, *querido*,' his mother inserted. 'You don't need his money. You don't need any of—'

'I don't want his damn money; I want to meet my half-brothers!' Anton lashed out, and watched his mother flinch, despised himself for it, despised Ramirez for doing this to them all. His mother was right, he didn't *need* to do anything. But, knowing that did not alter the fact that he felt bloody cheated—denied of the right to know so many things about himself.

He would *not* be denied this chance to know his own flesh and blood—no matter what the cost!

The cost.

His gaze flicked back to the papers spread out in front of him, green eyes glassing over as he re-read the paragraph in which Ramirez accused him of running out on a woman six years ago, leaving her in dire straits. He was insisting that Anton make reparation and was giving him six months in which to do it. He was then expected to turn up at some lawyer's office in Rio with this woman as his wife, ripe with his child, or he would never know his brothers and Anton's share in his birthright would go to *her* instead.

'So w-what are you going to do?' his mother questioned.

Anton didn't hear her. He was too busy staring at the name typed in bold print that was leaping at him off the page—along with a vision of waist-length black hair with a sexy loose spiral twist framing a small heart-shaped face with a pointed little chin, a lush red provocative mouth, and a pair of she-devil fiery dark eyes that had a habit of turning into burning rubies when she was—

'Anton…?'

His eyes lifted automatically at that appealing note in his mother's voice, but he wasn't seeing her because he was seeing that other woman who had been so instrumental in the making of him. His body was burning, filling with the deep grinding pulse of uncontrolled sexual power that had always been his response whenever he let—

'Anton, please tell us what you intend to do about this!' his mother begged.

'Carry out his wishes,' he heard himself utter, as cold and hard as death.

'What—get *married* at some dead man's behest?' his uncle Max gasped in horror. 'Are you crazy, boy?'

Stark staring mad—but up for it, Anton thought as the heat in him grew and grew. He was going to hunt down, trap and then marry the lying little tramp called Cristina Marques and make her life a sexual hell…

*   *   *

The old and sadly neglected book-lined room that had used to be her father's sanctuary rang to the sound of raised voices and the fierce-eyed fury of one of its two occupants.

'For goodness' sake, Cristina, will you listen to me? If you—'

'No, *you* listen.' A small clenched fist made angry contact with the desk. 'I said no!'

Sheer frustration threw Rodrigo Valentim back into his seat. 'If you will not take my instruction,' he sighed out impatiently, 'then what am I doing here?'

'You are here as my attorney to find a way to get me out of this!'

'And I keep telling you,' he enunciated tightly—but then this had been going on for ages now, and the longer it did the more angry both of them became— 'I cannot do that!'

Cristina straightened, her fine-boned slender figure giving no hint to the strength of the woman within. With a proud toss of her head she sent her long black tresses flying back from narrow shoulders. Eyes like flashing devils pierced Rodrigo Valentim with a defiant glare.

'Then I will have to find myself a lawyer who can, will I not?'

Another loaded sigh and Rodrigo's forty-years-in-the-business jaded expression suddenly gave way to a rueful smile. 'If I believed it could make the difference then I would take you to one myself. Do you not understand, *minha amiga*?' he pleaded. 'Santa Rosa is all but bankrupt. If you do not agree to this offer it will die!'

It was like taking a whip to a wounded animal. Cristina's pained little whimper crucified the tough lawyer's ears. She turned away, tense fingers jumping up to burrow into the sleeves of a well-used sweater as she paced away from the desk. The window beckoned, drawing her hopeless gaze to the open pampas, where the gauchos roamed free and machismo still ruled.

Out there, where most of the other large estates had turned their land over to soya or wine, Santa Rosa was one of the few traditional working cattle ranches left functioning in this part of Brazil. A Marques had ruled here since her Portuguese ancestors had claimed the land and built this house she was standing in.

And here she stood, Cristina thought bleakly, the last Marques in a long invincible line—and a female, of all things.

A female who was being forced to face the demise of the Marques land, name and pride.

'Your father should have let you run things years ago, then you would not be in this mess,' Rodrigo gruffly pronounced. 'He was a stubborn old fool.'

That word machismo echoed again, and Cristina's lovely mouth stretched into a bitter, wry smile. The men in these parts did not defer to their women. Her father had preferred to turn a blind eye to what was happening around him and wait to die rather than hand a single decision about Santa Rosa over to her.

'You need big investment to put this place back on its feet again,' Rodrigo continued. 'And you need it urgently. The Alagoas Consortium offer is more than generous for your purposes, *querida*.'

'At an *impossible* price.'

The consortium wanted to scythe off a whole section of Santa Rosa, which would give them access to part of a subtropical forest that was of particular natural beauty—not that this was what interested them. The forest blocked the rest of the world from mile upon mile of white sandy beaches, making them impossible to reach by land at present. They aimed to buy the tract of land, then bulldoze the forest and build a road link to the Atlantic, where they planned to build skyscrapers along a beautiful and rare stretch of untouched coast.

'When is there never a price?' Rodrigo posed sadly. 'You of all people should know this.'

Because she had paid a heavy price once before to save Santa Rosa. That 'price' was dead now, thank goodness. Along with the man who had been content to sell his daughter to gain a few extra years of comfort in his blindness to what was happening. Now here she stood with her eyes wide open, seeing all too clearly who must pay the price this time around. If she did accept the offer, the land, the people who lived on it and the forest would become the sacrifice.

'How long do I have to make a decision?' It stuck in her throat to ask the question and it showed in the husky tone of her voice.

'They want the deal badly enough to wait only a little while,' Rodrigo answered.

Cristina turned and nodded. 'Then keep them hanging on for their—little while,' she instructed. 'And I will make one last plea to the banks for help.'

'You have done this several times already.'

'And I will do it as many times as it takes until time runs out for me.'

'It is running out, Cristina,' Rodrigo said heavily. 'The wolves are already baying at your door.'

'I must still keep trying.' Dark eyes and soft mouth firm in their stubbornness, Cristina turned back to the window. Behind her, Rodrigo studied her too-slender figure with a kind of pained exasperation tinged with genuine but useless respect.

She was beautiful—exquisite—the kind of woman who at only twenty-five years old should have had the whole world lying at her feet. Indeed, she had once been that favoured person.

Then something had happened in this house to make her run away, and she had not been heard of again for over a year. When she eventually had come back she'd been a different person, hardened and cold, as if someone had snuffed out the burning light that had made her the wildly beautiful creature she had once been. She'd walked back into this house and within weeks out of it again, as the wife of Vaasco Ordoniz, a man as old as the father who had happily sold her to him.

For the next year she had lived in Rio as a rich old man's beautiful ornament. She'd outfaced her critics and their bitching cruelty without a hint of her true feelings showing on her face. When Ordoniz had taken sick and retired from society to his isolated ranch he'd taken Cristina with him, and neither had been seen or heard of for the next two years. Then Ordoniz had died, and the mocking laughter had truly been heard when it had come to light that he'd been quietly gambling his wealth away, leaving his fortune-chasing wife so penniless she'd had to move back to her father's house to become unpaid servant and nurse to yet another sick, money-squandering old man.

Yet her stubborn chin had never faltered. Those beautiful eyes had always looked out on life with defiance and pride. Rodrigo admired her for those things and respected her refusal to give up on life no matter how many bad things it threw at her.

'Okay, we will give it one more try,' he heard himself utter, and wondered straight away if he was being cruel to offer her a small chink of light? 'I think we will enlist some help this time. Gabriel knows all the right people.' He did not add that his son had already been approached by some anonymous businessman looking for new investment in

Brazil. Rodrigo did not want to raise her hopes. 'Gabriel just might be able to get you a hearing with those who would not listen to you before.'

Still, when Cristina turned to look at him, her hopes were already rising in the new shine in her eyes.

Rodrigo heaved a sigh. 'Gabriel might run in the right circles, Cristina, but money men are notoriously ruthless. They will not invest in you without demanding something solid back in return.'

CHAPTER TWO

ANTON saw him as he was crossing the hotel foyer, and on a single heavy thump of a heartbeat he came to an abrupt halt.

It had been happening a lot since he'd been told he had two half-brothers out there. He would glimpse a man with dark hair, or with something about his physical appearance that reminded him of himself, and this thump at his heart would stop him in his tracks.

It was the not knowing that made it impossible to deal with—the deep-boned fear that he could be standing right next to his own flesh and blood and not have a single clue.

He hated it. He hated this sudden leap his heart would make just before the thick sinking rush that paralysed him.

And the need—he hated feeling this need he hadn't known was there until he'd received that damn—

'Anton…?'

Kinsella's questioning prompt jolted him back to his surroundings. The stranger had gone, disappearing into one of the lounge bars and out of Anton's sphere of temptation to just go up to him and ask outright if his father had been a rich polo-playing Brazilian who'd left bastard byeblows in just about every port!

Anger set him moving again, though it did not show on his face. They hit the lifts, four of them in all, the two junior executives looking limp with jet-lag while Kinsella, his new personal secretary, who had only recently been promoted through the Scott-Lee ranks, still looked as smooth and fresh as she had all day.

Anton glanced at her and she thoroughly jolted him by offering him one of those smiles that said *I'm available if you want me*. She was a great-looking blue-eyed blonde, with the kind of figure guaranteed to fire up most men's heat. Until now she'd been good to have around because she was easy on the eye and her secretarial skills were unquestionable—but sex with the boss as a sideline?

He lowered his eyes and pretended he had not noticed the invitation—or the sudden tension that leapt around the confines of the lift. Apart from the unbroken rule that he never bedded his employees, he hadn't wanted to touch a woman since the day when his life as he'd known it had been put to death.

The lift doors slid open. His two junior executives quickly stepped out into the corridor, eager to find their rooms, but Kinsella left it a couple of telling seconds longer before she did the same.

Once again Anton ignored the little hesitation. Eyes half hidden behind the low sweep of his eyelashes he said, 'Get some food inside you, then sleep off the jet-lag. I'll see you all for breakfast in my suite at seven-thirty prompt.'

The boss playing the boss, he noted wryly, as three heads nodded, getting the message, one looking faintly flushed now. Serves you right, Kinsella, he thought, without a twinge of regret.

'Goodnight,' he said, and the lift doors slid shut across their three murmured replies.

Anton yawned, stuffed his hands into his trouser pockets and leant back against the lift wall as it took him up to the penthouse suite on the top floor, where not only did he get the best in accommodation that was available, but he also got adjoining offices and a conference room in which most of his business day would be spent.

He preferred working from his hotel when he made

an unannounced spot-check on one of his international branches. That way he could sweep into the bank and take everyone by surprise, so that they did not have time to pull any cover-ups. He would then put every department head through a major grilling before sweeping out again, with his entourage in tow, and returning to his hotel to hold his post mortem, leaving his quivering staff to recover from the fallout of his unexpected invasion. They would call him a few tasty names to each other, enjoy a collective sigh of relief that he'd gone. Then they would start urgently boning up on what they'd thought they knew inside out but, after one of Anton's interrogating sessions, had now realised they knew nothing at all.

Ruthless but necessary methods to keep his multinational army of employees on their toes, he judged without a qualm.

The lift doors slid open again. Levering himself upright, he crossed the private foyer and unlocked the door. The suite was much like any other hotel suite he had used over the years, with luxurious living space, two bedrooms with *en suite* bathrooms, and a connecting door which led directly into the all-singing, all-dancing working environment business tycoons expected from their accommodation these days.

His luggage had arrived. Ignoring it, Anton made directly for the drinks cabinet to check that the hotel had provided him with a bottle of his favourite Scotch whisky. He poured himself a measure, added some bottled water to the mix, then took it with him to a pair of French doors which led out onto a terrace beyond.

The moment he stepped outside, the sights and sounds of Rio hit his senses, stirring them to a quickened rhythm only someone with Latin blood running through him would understand.

That quickened rhythm should be filling him with pleasure, but it wasn't. In fact he resented the hell out of it. It was six long years since he'd last looked out on the Bay towards Sugarloaf, and if he'd had his way it would have been another six years before he'd look out on it again—if ever.

He took a sip of the whisky, the shape of his sensually moulded lips barely altering their grim tilt as they parted to receive the drink. Heat rolled over his tongue and fired up his increased pulse-beat. He'd used to love Rio de Janeiro. This beautiful, exciting city had once been like a home from home to him during his childhood, when he'd used to visit here regularly with his mother, and later, when he'd spent a full year working at the Scott-Lee Bank branch here.

With hindsight, he mused, he would have been better staying put in England, then he would not have met Cristina and spent that whole year in love with a lie.

Another lie.

That hot surge of anger he'd been nurturing for weeks now began to pump through his system. Going back inside, he closed the door on the sights and sounds of Rio, chose a bedroom at random to use, then set about removing his clothes. Ten minutes later he was shutting down the taps gushing water into a huge sunken bathtub.

The tub needed to be big to accommodate a man with his impressive framework. He stood six feet two in his bare feet, and every inch was made up of hard muscled bulk. And lean, he was very lean, but that leanness did not take anything away from the fact that, stripped to his natural golden skin, he presented the kind of masculine sight that could make women gasp. Wide shoulders, long torso, narrow hips, the lot supported on long and powerfully corded legs. Then there was the pelvis that cradled one of the major weapons in his sexual arsenal. He was built to seduce, built to guarantee hours of untold pleasure. He knew it—just as his women knew it.

Not that he cared about any of that right now as he stepped into the bath and sank down into its hot steamy depths. He was tired and fed up and still wishing himself elsewhere. Easing his wide shoulders back against the bath, he closed his eyes on a sigh.

If it wasn't enough that he'd seen the interior of too damn many transit lounges as he'd criss-crossed the world to get here, he'd spent most of that time obsessively studying every tall dark guy that ventured into his vicinity, hunting for signs that one of them might be related to him.

He hated the not knowing.

He more than hated Rio.

If he'd been given the luxury of choice he'd rather be anywhere else on this earth than here. But choice was something snatched away from him by the simple insertion of a name.

Cristina Marques...

The satin gold muscular formation of his wide shoulders shifted, black silk bars for eyebrows drawing together across the bridge of his nose. Parting the grim tension holding his lips together, he gritted his teeth and wished to hell that other parts of his body would stop responding to that name.

Another sigh had him lifting a wet hand to swipe it over his tired face. The refreshing sting of hot water made his skin tingle, but did nothing to ease the discomfort of a twelve-hour beard growth. He should have shaved before he got in here, he mused grimly. He should have cleaned his teeth.

The second thought sent his hand reaching out in search of the glass of whisky he'd had enough sense to replenish before he climbed in here. Sipping the Scotch was a darn sight tastier than any toothpaste, and did a whole lot more to ease the tension from his aching muscles—though not from other parts.

What he needed was a woman—any woman. He hadn't had one in way too long. He'd been too busy losing himself in work and bad temper and setting up this trip. A woman right now might just be the medicine he needed to effect the cure for the one woman he did not want to want.

Maybe he should have broken his own rule and taken Kinsella up on her offer, he mused idly. Maybe a slender, sleek, blue-eyed blonde would be the perfect cure for what was ailing him. But—

No. He might have closed the door on the sights and sounds of Rio, but its innate beat was still vibrating through his blood, and the only woman who would satisfy it would have to be one of the warm, dark, passionate kind. One who would know instinctively that all he wanted her to do was to climb naked into this bath with him and seduce him to one of those exquisite near death experiences.

A half smile touched the edges of his mouth, his shoulders beginning to relax as he let his weary mind drift. She would have a pair of decent-sized breasts that would weigh heavy in his hands but still be firm enough to pout. Dark nipples…he loved dark nipples…and a silky, slippery golden body that would arch over him in pleasure as he suckled to his heart's content.

His mouth received attention from the whisky. It wasn't nearly the same as the glorious sense-tugging taste of a woman, but he savoured it all the same while behind closed eyelids his fantasy woman began to take real shape.

Dark eyes…she'd have sultry dark eyes the colour of hunger, and sweeping black eyelashes that would half hide the glow of sensual relish she would experience as she aroused him while he lay back and enjoyed. Ebony hair, he decided, with a sexy hint of a twist to it that would trail over his chest and shoulders as she leant down to offer him a kiss from her gorgeous, greedy, voluptuous mouth, practised in the art of pleasing as she took him inside her with the…

'Hell—'

The curse raked his throat and he sat up so abruptly he spilled whisky into the bath. He'd been describing Cristina. He'd been lying here flirting with fantasy and building himself the perfect replica of the one woman he was supposed to be blocking out!

Tell that to your body, he thought darkly, and rid himself of the glass, then rubbed his wet hands over his face again. Tension had hold of him in a manacle. Standing up, he dripped water from taut rippling muscles as he stepped out of the bath. As he hooked up a towel to dry himself, it accidentally brushed across that part of him that was an aching agony of untamed want. With an indrawn quiver of cursing contempt, he tossed the towel aside and headed for a cold shower instead.

He didn't want to want Cristina. He did not want to remember how she was. He wanted to be utterly turned off by reality, and hoped that when he eventually came face to face with her she'd have turned into a complete hound dog!

And he would come face to face with her, he vowed as he stepped out of the shower cubicle feeling more like a man in control of himself. The wheels to make it happen were already turning, and very soon he would have his confrontation with Cristina Marques.

The telephone began ringing as he was finishing shaving. Walking naked out of the bathroom, he picked up the receiver.

'I have tracked her to Rio, *senhor*,' a distinctly Brazilian male voice informed him. 'She is residing with Gabriel Valentim. He will be escorting her to the charity gala tomorrow evening, as hoped.'

She was hooked; the sting was on. The hot burn of satisfaction that flung itself down his body excited a sexual arousal he had thought he'd brought under control.

'Good,' he said, as cold as an English winter. 'Tell me the rest tomorrow.'

'Before you go there is something I have discovered that I think you should know, *senhor*!' Afonso Sanchiz put in hurriedly. 'It was not mentioned in the profile you sent to me—but six years ago the lady in question married a man called Vaasco Ordoniz. She is widowed now, and has reverted to using the Marques name, but...'

Cristina did not want to be here. Partying while her life was tumbling down around her placed a very bad taste in her mouth. But Gabriel insisted it was the only way. The best deals were struck in the social arena, not across a desk in some bank.

So here she was, standing in the foyer of one of Rio's top hotels, dressed to kill in sparkling black silk. Her hair was up in an elegant twist and her late mother's diamonds sparkled at her ears and throat.

She would have sold the diamonds if they'd been worth anything, but she'd found out the hard way that they were not. They were fakes—very good fakes, but fakes all the same. She did not know when her father had cashed in the genuine articles and replaced them with paste, but she had little doubt that he had done so. In fact, she'd discovered over the months since he died that there was very little left in Santa Rosa that was not a copy of its original. She now lived with the hope that when Lorenco Marques met his art-collecting ancestors on his way up to heaven they'd give him a swift push in the other direction.

And, yes, she told that shocked part of her that did not like what she was thinking, she felt that bitter and that bad.

Gabriel was guiding her towards a pair of doors beyond which the charity gala they were about to attend should be in full flow. Two smiling lackeys jumped to open the doors for them. The smooth background sound of a bossa nova song drifted out towards them as the foyer gave way to a vast reception room set against a backcloth of wall-to-wall glass, offering breathtaking views towards a night-lit Sugarloaf.

People glittered and sparkled beneath overhead lighting, the warm tones of their conversations floating towards her on richly perfumed waves. Cristina's stomach lurched, then rolled, and for a moment her courage completely failed her, pulling her to a trembling halt.

From the other side of the room Anton watched as she entered on the arm of just about the most attractive man here. She was still unutterably beautiful, he noted, allowing himself a small grimace at his unanswered hound dog prayer. The hair was too neat for his liking, and the dress might be glamorous, and sexy enough to knock most men's eyes out, but he'd never liked to see her wearing black. She suited bright colours, colours that flagged her hot-blooded temperament. But the face, the wide-spaced almond-shaped eyes, the mouth…

Ah, the mouth, he observed darkly. It was still as lush and red and kissable as he remembered it. A mouth that instinctively knew how to—

Her escort murmured something to her. As she looked up to smile at him sudden tension was bathing Anton's body in a fine layer of sensual heat. It was the smile of a born seductress. A smile she had once used to keep exclusively for him. It was the deceit in that smile that had ruined all other smiles every woman had offered him since.

Did she sleep with Gabriel Valentim? Had the handsome lawyer got to share a steamy hot interlude in a bath with the widow of Vaasco Ordoniz before they'd set out here?

'Anton, your glass is empty...'

Looking down, he saw it was, frowning slightly because he didn't remember drinking the champagne. He must have been sipping it while observing Cristina with her latest lover. Now he became aware of the tension in the fingers that held the glass and the angry fizz of champagne in his mouth.

'Here, let me replace it...'

Reaching out, Kinsella took the empty glass from him. As she did so her body brushed against his. She was wearing no bra beneath the slip dress she was wearing. He'd felt the button-tight brush of her nipple against the back of his hand.

Yet another sexual message from his secretary? Irritation hit, then was instantly lost when he caught sight of Cristina's escort lowering his handsome head to brush a kiss to her cheek.

'Stop worrying,' Gabriel softly chided her, feeling the tension in the stiff set of her spine beneath the resting palm of his hand. 'No one is going to eat you.'

No? Cristina would question that. Six years ago she had scandalised these people by marrying a man old enough to be her father. She had become a gold-digging freak worthy of derision and scorn from that moment on. Discovering that Vaasco Ordoniz had left her virtually penniless would not have altered their opinion of his widow.

A waiter appeared, carrying a silver tray of drinks.

'Here.' Hooking up two fluted glasses frothing with

champagne Gabriel slotted one into her hand. 'Remember why you are here,' he said firmly. 'Get some of this fortifying champagne inside you and stop looking so tragic.'

'I am not in any way tragic,' Cristina denied, trying hard to ignore the hectic thrum of her pulse. 'I just dislike the prospect of having to be pleasant to people I no longer like.'

'Does that include me?'

Glancing up into the lean golden face of the man she had known since childhood, Cristina saw the wry glint of amusement in his soft amber eyes and couldn't help but smile.

'Thank you for doing this for me,' she said softly. 'I know that your father had to push you into it.'

'I don't need pushing to be with a beautiful woman, *querida*.' Reaching out, he covered her fingers and lifted the glass to her lips, then held it there until she took the first sip. 'And you should know better than to think that I am one of those who believed the gold-digging rumours about you.'

Her smile faded. 'Would it make a difference if I told you that those rumours were true?'

'To my escorting you?' Gabriel's mouth assumed a small grimace. 'Look at these people, Cristina,' he prompted. 'Do you think none of them have skeletons to hide? I am a lawyer, like my father. Such a profession allows access to privileged information that would make the hair on the head of the good father in the confessional box stand on end. Take my advice and look upon them all as crooks and you will begin to feel much better about yourself.'

Her eyes widened in fascination. '*Are* they all crooks?'

'No.' Gabriel laughed. 'But it helps a great deal to see them like that.'

Someone came up to greet Gabriel then, a perfect

stranger to Cristina, so she was able to relax a little as Gabriel made the introductions and even managed to smile as she sipped at her glass of champagne and listened to the two men converse. A few minutes later the stranger had moved off again, and they began to circulate.

Gabriel's hand was always light on her waistline. He was well known and well liked, his good looks and his naturally friendly manner drew people to him, and she wanted to kiss him for the way he was carefully manoeuvring them around the room so that she was not forced to come face to face with any of the old crowd—though she had glimpsed many of them here.

It was then that it happened. Just as she was beginning to relax in the company she picked up the sound of a dark-timbred very English voice, speaking in such beautifully fluent Portuguese that she had twisted around without giving herself a chance to think.

By then it was too late. Her swift movement had caught his attention. The next instant she found herself welded to the spot as a pair of darkly hooded glinting green eyes fixed on her shocked face.

Luis, she thought. *Meu Dues*, it was Luis…

He was standing less than ten feet away, a tall, lean, solid, dark force backed by the night view of Rio. Her legs turned to water, her head swirling so dizzily that for a horrible moment she was afraid that she was actually going to faint. No one else was in the room suddenly. No voices sounded. No slow and sensual bossa nova beat. All she could hear was the blood pumping heavily through her body as those hooded eyes looked at her and took everything, stripping away six long miserable years to leave her standing there feeling so exposed and vulnerable that she just could not bring herself to look away.

And he wasn't going to do it, she realised as she watched

those eyes begin a slow, slow glide over her face. Her shock-blackened eyes. Her shock-whitened cheeks. He let his gaze linger on every telling detail until finally fixing it on her helplessly parted lips.

Those lips quivered as if he'd touched them. A knowing smile stretched the contours of his. It was electric, dynamic, so overwhelmingly sexual and intensely familiar she was nailed by it, drenched in sensation that slithered and danced across her skin. They had been lovers for twelve months more than six years ago, yet for these few breathtaking seconds those years just did not exist.

She trembled—all over. He watched that happen too, and swung his gaze up to clash with hers again. Mockery lanced through those glinting green eyes and he lifted his glass, tilting it towards her in a salute that was so dryly cynical it sucked her back through those six years with a painful, dizzying whoosh.

He hated her. It was there for her to see it. And she could not even blame him for feeling that way. She had encouraged him to hate—worked at it like an actress putting on an Oscar-winning performance. She'd mocked him and cursed him and died a little more inside with each slaying remark she had thrown at his face.

Tears began to gather, hot, like acid burning in her chest and her throat. She loved him, would always love him for as long as she had left to draw breath, but she'd wished— oh, how she had wished—never to set eyes on him again.

Someone shifted beside him, forcing her gaze to flicker sideways in time to watch a woman step in close to murmur something to him. She was beautiful, a reed-slender blonde wearing aquamarine silk. Whatever it was that she said to Luis, it lost Cristina her contact with his eyes as he turned to the woman with a lazy, sensual smile on his lips.

And Cristina knew that smile, recognised it with every sensory nerve she possessed. They were lovers. Jealousy roared up like a snarling, spitting wild animal inside her, and on a choked little whimper she spun away.

Trembling like mad, she moved in so close to Gabriel that she earned herself a curious glance as his arm accommodated her, though his attention did not falter from the discussion he was involved in.

'The problem has been global,' he was saying smoothly. 'But the industry is showing signs of recovery, and we have a plan in place to get in first where this growth is happening. People will pay a high price for a flawless pedigree. Santa Rosa can give them that—hmm, Cristina?' He prompted some input from her.

Gabriel was into his sales pitch, and she had to fight a gigantic battle with herself to find sensible words to speak.

'S-Santa Rosa stock is conceived born and raised on the land on which it roams free,' she heard herself say, as if from down a long dark tunnel. 'We are proud that we still farm by traditional methods where quality always takes precedence over quantity.'

'But quantity is what makes the big profit, *senhorita*,' Gabriel's companion wryly pointed out.

'*Sim.*' She nodded, battling to keep herself together. 'We know this, which is why we want to diversify a little…turn Santa Rosa into a showcase where people can come and stay for a while, experience what it is like to live in a genuine Portuguese mansion house, and spend time with the gauchos learning of the life and true traditions of a working ranch. But such plans require investment—'

'At great risk to the investor, I would say,' a smooth-as-silk voice put in.

Both Gabriel and his companion turned to face the newcomer. Cristina didn't—not again, she told herself as her pounding heart increased its crazy beat.

'Most worthy investments require a certain amount of risk, *senhor*,' Gabriel countered easily.

'The knack for the successful investor is to pick out those investments that have at least a starting chance to earn him some profit.'

'With commitment to hard work and true dedication we can certainly promise our investors their profit,' Gabriel declared without hesitation, at the same time making out that he had a big stake in the project himself, when in truth he was simply playing the machismo rule to the hilt for her sake. 'Let me introduce myself,' he then offered affably, releasing Cristina to hold out his hand. 'I am Gabriel Valentim, and this is—'

'I know who this is…' Anton smoothly put in, and the instant that Gabriel's hand left the base of her spine his replaced it, fingertips moving in an all too familiar stroke that sent shock waves stinging up her spine.

His warm breath brushed her nape as he moved in closer. 'Cristina, *meu querida*,' he greeted with husky intimacy. 'Surely you must remember me?'

It took every ounce of will power she could muster to turn and face him. Her insides were dipping and diving even before she lifted her chin and looked directly into his face.

'Luis,' she responded, with very shaky coolness.

'But you're mistaken,' a cool English voice intruded. 'This is Anton—Anton Scott-Lee.'

Anton Luis Ferreira Scott-Lee, to give him his full title, Cristina corrected silently. Anton to most people, but always Luis to her. A man with two faces—his English face and his Brazilian face.

And she was seeing his Brazilian face right now, as he

smiled one of his slow, sensual smiles at her and reached out to take a light grasp on her hand. 'Don't look so shattered,' he softly admonished. 'I will answer to Luis if it still pleases you to use it…'

The air in her lungs ceased to be of any use to her. This close up he was everything she remembered about him— everything. Her lips parted, trembling again as she tried desperately to find something light to say.

'This is some kind of joke, yes?' Gabriel asked curiously, as a set of slender white fingers claimed Cristina's attention by coiling possessively around Luis' sleeve.

The fingers belonged to his beautiful blonde companion. Cristina glanced into a pair of gentian-blue eyes and blinked at the amount of ice she met with. Was this the kind of woman Luis preferred these days?

'No joke,' the man himself was denying, bringing Cristina's eyes slewing back to his face. 'Cristina and I are very old friends—hmm, *amante*?'

Lover.

Her senses went haywire. She had to fight to pull in some air, unaware of the silence slowly thickening around them, unaware of everything but those eyes and that smile and that *word*, playing like a silken caress across her skin.

A thumb-pad stroked against the skin of her palm and she looked down at it, staring blankly at the way his long fingers coiled so easily around the fragility of hers.

'Cristina?' Gabriel prompted an answer from her, because she was taking too long to speak.

She looked up at him next, not seeing him—not seeing anything. Not even the flash of venom that hit Luis's companion's eyes. Her heart had stopped beating. The thick curdling slurry of so many old feelings was churning inside her, leeching the last of the colour from her skin. She couldn't think. Even as she tried very hard to find the right response that would defuse the tense moment a thick whooshing sound in her head stopped her from being able to think.

His thumb stroked her palm again and she looked back at her hand, still caught in his. She felt a strange lethargy creep over her, and on a shivered gasp tugged her hand free.

'I—please excuse me,' she heard herself mumble in stifled constriction. 'I n-need to—use the bathroom...'

And on that crass, stupid and utterly unsophisticated exit line she turned and fled, leaving a stunning silence in her place.

On legs that felt dangerously like cotton wool she made it into the foyer. A passing waiter had only to take one look at her face to quickly direct her to the nearest private bathroom. Closing the door behind her, she leant back against it. She was shaking all over, locked in the kind of hard shock that turned flesh to ice. Lurching unsteadily across the room, she sank down onto the toilet seat.

Luis was here in Rio. *'Meu dues,'* she whispered.

Why was he here? Why now, after all of these years? Why should he want to acknowledge her at all?

It came then, that final damning scene they'd had six years ago, swimming up through her mind to send her hands up to cover her face. She saw Luis standing there, stunned and bewildered, staring at her as if she had grown a forked tail and hooves.

'What's wrong with you? You love me. Why are you doing this? We lived here together for a year before I had to go back to England to attend my father's funeral. That year must have meant something to you—told you that I was serious about us!'

'Things change—' He'd been too angry to notice her deathly pallor, or the agony etched into her face.

'In three months? No, they don't,' he'd denied harshly. 'You made me promise to come back for you and here I am as promised, with a rock-solid marriage proposal and plane tickets to a whole new life! For goodness' sake, Cristina—' his voice had roughened '—I love you. I want you to be my wife, I want to have children with you and grow old with you, watch those children grow into adults and have their own children!'

Cut to death inside by his vision of the future, she'd tossed her head at him. Sitting here in this room lined in glaring white marble, Cristina winced as she remembered the way she'd tossed her head at him that day. 'I will never marry you, Luis. I will never have your children. There, I have said it. Will you accept it now?'

Oh, yes, he'd accepted it. Cristina had seen it happen as she'd watched the bitter look that overtook his face. 'Because you don't want to spoil that perfect body of yours?'

'That is exactly it,' she'd agreed. 'I am selfish and heartless and incurably vain. I am also a Marques, with three centuries of pure Portuguese blood running in my veins. Diluting my blood with your half-English blood would be a sin and a sacrilege that would turn my ancestors in their—'

The brief knock on the door was the only warning she received before it was swinging open. Cristina lifted her face out of her hands, and froze yet again.

CHAPTER THREE

LUIS was not so afflicted. He shut the door and shot home the bolt she had stupidly forgotten when she'd come in here. Then he turned, leant his wide shoulders back against the door, pushed long-fingered hands into the pockets of his well-cut trousers, fixed his steady gaze on her agonised face and simply waited for her to make the next move.

Dressed in a dark lounge suit and white shirt he looked big and hard and absolutely in control. The room was too small, too brightly lit, and he was too close for comfort, the electric charge vibrating from every pore of him so violently sexual it grabbed her attention and refused to let go.

Mouth running dry, she took in every hard, honed inch of him like someone seeing the chance of life restoring water after a six year drought. Nothing about him had changed—nothing. His hair was still short black and silky, his skin still golden and smooth. Eyes the colour of a sensual green ocean glowed at her from between half lowered eyelashes, and the unsmiling shape of his mouth did nothing to spoil the passionate promise it made.

'When you fled in here like a frightened rabbit I knew you would forget to lock the door, because you always did forget to lock doors, so I thought—why not join her and relive some of the good old times?' he drawled.

Her insides quivering madly, Cristina lurched unsteadily to her feet, fingers searching for and clutching tensely at the sink behind her for support. 'W-what do you want?' she demanded shakily.

37

'Now, there's a good question.' The twist of his mouth was dryly sardonic as he sent his mocking gaze around the room. 'We could fill the room with hot steam, if you like, strip off our clothes and get down to some really physical reacquainting?' he suggested. 'I can see by the way you look at me that you're up for it, *querida*, and I'm certainly up for it. So what the hell?' He gave a shrug of his wide shoulders. 'We could do it against the bath, *in* the bath, in the shower, or right where you were sitting just now. Or you could coax me down flat on the cold marble floor like an offering and crawl all over me. You used to like crawling all over me, Cristina, do you remember? You used to love to make me beg, then laugh in my face as you took me inside you. *Got you, Luis,* you used to purr in that greedily possessive, husky, triumphant voice of yours. *Mine,* you used to say.'

'Shut up!' she gasped out shrilly. 'How dare you speak to me like this? Get out of here, Luis—*get out!*'

He did the opposite, pushing those muscled shoulders away from the door and striding forward so purposefully that Cristina found herself pressing back hard against the sink. It was like being trapped in a cage with a lean, dark green-eyed predator. She had never felt so afraid.

'No,' she breathed as a set of long fingers closed over a bare shoulder.

The other set lifted to curl around her nape. As she arched her back in an effort to put space between them he stepped in close. The solid bar of his hips made contact with her stomach. She quivered. He smiled—then stopped smiling. His eyes glittered, his lips parted, then he tugged her head forward and captured her mouth.

The predator—the predator—the *hungry* predator. She was devoured without mercy, lips prised apart and her mouth invaded by the kind of kiss that locked every muscle tight with shock. Her mouth filled with the taste of him, sensitive tissue untouched for too long pulsing with pleasure and crying out for more. He explored her teeth, the excruciatingly sensitive roof of her mouth, her fiercely retracted tongue.

Long fingers stroked across the satin skin of her shoulder, then slid to her back, to begin a slow gliding down the length of her spine. She was quivering all over by the time he heaved her tight up against him. The heady scent of him, the sensual knowledge of his touch, the unholy eroticism of his kiss wiped away six years without having to try hard, and as her arms lifted up and around his neck she marked her surrender to him with a pained little moan.

After that they were kissing like sex-starved wild things, hotly, deeply. It was mad. Moving against each other, heaving and panting, gripping and clawing—or she was. Anything—*anything*—to keep this from stopping. The heels of her shoes were screeching against marble, her fingers clutching at his silk dark head. Her skirt had rucked up round her hips, aided by the seeking slide of his hand, and he was touching with the intimate familiarity of a passionate lover—her thighs, the tight curve of her bottom—pressing her legs that bit wider to accept the taut, probing thrust of his manhood, straining against the zip of his trousers, while she tasted him, clung to him, moved and invited him.

It was desire gone rocketing out of control. She was hot, yet shivering, appalled with herself, yet desperate for more.

'Now?' he posed softly. 'You want it right here and now, *viuva de Ordoniz?*'

The widow Ordoniz. It was an icy douche that brought her gasping back down to earth.

Opening her eyes, she found he was standing there studying her through eyes that were cynical and cold. Oh, he was aroused. She could feel the power and strength of that arousal pushing against her. But the man himself was in complete control.

Unlike her.

His hand still claimed the heated dampness of her arousal. Shame had her push it away, only to release a revealing shudder at its removal. He found it so easy to let go and take a step back that she wanted to die where she stood.

'Who do you think you are to treat me this way?' she choked out, desperately tugging at the hem of her dress.

'The bit of rough you are clearly still partial to,' he answered, watching her go pale as his cutting reference hit home. Then he turned away. 'Now, pull yourself together.' It was hard and cold. 'We need to talk and we don't have much time.'

He glanced at his watch as he said that, not a crease on him, not a hair out of place. While she was a sizzling, quivering wreck he was a man so completely contained that tears of self-disgust stung at the backs of her eyes.

'We have nothing to talk about.' She just wanted him to get out of here.

'Oh, we do,' he turned to insist. 'You are in deep trouble, Cristina, not least because I am back in town. But we will deal with that some other time. I have a proposition to put to you.'

'I want nothing to do with you.'

'But you will by the end of this evening,' he assured her with cool confidence. 'And stop looking at me as if I'm some kind of snake because you find that you're still hot for me. It's in your favour that you do feel like that, or I would be leaving you to the hungry wolves out there.'

'I don't know what you are talking about.'

'Yes, you do. And sticking that defiant chin up to me

and firing contempt from those eyes won't cut it,' he sliced at her deridingly. 'You always were a skilled little liar—and you do know what I am talking about now, I see…'

His eyes raked her face as it paled with understanding.

'Yes.' He smiled. 'You made a big mistake six years ago when you tossed me aside with your lies and then trotted off to marry an old man with one foot already in his grave. You should have listened more closely to me when I told you how much I was worth. Even my unworthy half-English blood has a sweet taste to it when it comes wrapped in billions, *amante*. Now look at you,' he mocked. 'A pariah in your so-precious Portuguese society. And look at me, the half Englishman, holding the only chance you will have to save your Marques pride.'

'You are not the only rich financier here tonight,' Cristina hit back, wanting to sink weakly back down on the toilet seat and keeping herself upright only with the help of that Marques pride he'd just tried to crucify.

Beautiful, Anton thought. Sensational—exciting. Even while she stands there still trying to kill me with her eyes. And, yes, I'm up for it, he reaffirmed angrily. Whatever the lying sob story that was fed to Enrique Ramirez about our relationship six years ago, I am willing to fulfil his conditions and marry the Ordoniz widow. I'll fill her up with my seed and I will make reparation to *myself*, by never telling her how that seed is as Portuguese as her own.

Revenge, he decided, will taste sweet.

'By all means spend the rest of the evening taking your begging bowl round the present company,' he invited. 'You never know—you might get lucky and snag some other old man willing to bail you out in exchange for the use of that perfect body of yours. But if the bowl remains empty, then call this number…' Taking a business card out of his pocket, Anton handed it to her. 'It has my private line via the hotel switchboard,' he explained as she stared down at the card embossed with the logo of a top hotel in Rio. 'And remember, *querida*, when you do use that number, to ask for *Anton* Scott-Lee—not *Luis*.'

With that cutting stab at the other intimacy they had shared, he turned and walked to the door, unbolted it and walked out, leaving Cristina staring numbly after him as the door slid quietly back into its housing.

Silence clattered down. She began shaking all over, shock overlaying the skin-burning residue of his touch, holding her still as she listened to the sound of his deep voice as he began speaking to someone in the foyer, advising them to find another bathroom because this one was broken.

'Believe me, you really don't want to go in there,' she heard him say in smoothly amused cultivated English which brought forth a fluttering flirtatious female laugh that for some silly reason flooded her eyes with hot tears.

When he turned on that voice he could charm anyone, she remembered. He'd charmed her into his life and into his bed without having to try very hard.

For an impressionable young woman up from the country used only to meeting the dow old friends of her father or solitary gauchos out on the plains, Luis had been like a fairytale figure to her—young, handsome, light-hearted, passionate, and so exciting to be with he'd turned her escape to Rio into the most magical time of her life.

And she'd loved him totally. Still loved him like that, she admitted as a second wave of pained tears burnt her eyes. When she'd thrown Luis away so callously she'd thrown her heart away with him, and lived the last six years without one.

The shared laughter on the other side of the door grew

quieter as they moved away, then there was silence. With an effort Cristina pulled herself together, turning to check her hair and her make-up in the mirror and hurriedly trying to cover the swollen evidence of his kiss with a layer of red lipstick. It was not successful—how could it be when her lips continued to pulse, her eyes shone too brightly and her skin wore a flush that was not all to do with humiliation and shame?

She looked away, turned away, then took in a deep breath and made herself go back to the party—to hear from a disgruntled Gabriel that Luis had already left with his beautiful companion.

'Where do you know him from? How did you meet him?' he demanded to know. 'Do you know *who* he is? He owns big stakes in just about every banking house between here and the moon, and if I had known you knew him we could have used the connection. But the way you just walked away has probably blown that opportunity.'

'Sorry,' she murmured, not sorry at all. 'I felt ill suddenly. I thought you would prefer it if I didn't embarrass you by throwing up on his shoes.'

The begging bowl remained empty. By the time Gabriel saw Cristina into his car, the mood between them had turned very grim. As he drove them towards his apartment the silence grew like a heavy weight around both of them.

Then he told her why. 'The word is out, Cristina. You are untouchable. Most of the people there tonight have a stake in the Alagoas Consortium. They *want* you to surrender and sell.'

Strangely enough, she was not surprised—though she did wonder how big a stake Luis was holding.

It was the first question she asked him when she rang him from the privacy of the bedroom Gabriel had loaned her for her stay in Rio. She'd left Gabriel stretched out on a chair in his living room, brooding about the evening over a glass of brandy before going out again to meet up with his lover.

'Is it relevant?' Luis countered.

'If you want to see me fail as much as everyone else does, then yes,' she said. 'It is relevant.'

'Be here at my suite at twelve o'clock sharp,' was all he said. 'And don't bother to bring the lover along with you.'

'Lover?' she echoed blankly.

'The handsome blond with the very white teeth,' he extended with a sarcastic bite from his own white teeth.

'You mean Gabriel?'

'Yes, I mean Gabriel,' he mocked her.

'But he is—'

'Out, *querida*,' Anton said coldly. 'And I mean right out—of your life *and* the business loop. If you want me to save your precious Santa Rosa then from now on you deal only and exclusively with me.'

The line went dead. Anton let the receiver fall onto his naked chest and released a surprised laugh.

She'd cut him off, the reckless little witch!

The laugh changed into a smile as he relaxed back on to the pillows to stare at the ceiling while he imagined the way her eyes would be flashing with fury right now. He might have her cornered, shocked and frightened, but he had not scared her enough to make her behave herself when she was angry.

Nobody told Cristina Marques what to do. The moment anyone attempted to lay down the law with her she turned into a she-devil with bite. She got fiery and feisty and sometimes totally, excitingly unmanageable. They'd had rows in their twelve months together that had made Rio shake. She'd slammed doors, spat insults and all but lit up with defiance—while he had remained so laid back and cool about everything it had used to send her wilder still.

He'd used to love her wildness. He'd used to stand back and calmly goad her on, then wait for the moment when she would fly at him with her angry claws drawn. Fielding her with the ease of a man virtually born on an English rugby field had been a delight and a provocation in itself. She would kick, she would bite, she would scratch—or try to, without a hope of wounding him. And he would urge her on with taunts from his eyes and provoking comments while he went looking for the nearest horizontal surface on which to safely drop her.

And himself. Of course himself. A wide naked shoulder gave a shrug as if that was a given. You didn't catch yourself a wild thing without enjoying all of that fire and passion. You tapped into it. You provoked it further. You let it drive you crazy until that defining moment arrived when—

The phone rang again, vibrating against the smattering of dark hair on his chest. He lifted it to his ear.

'You will not dictate to me, Luis!' Her voice came shrill, packed with those sensationally sexy vowel sounds that littered her English. 'This is business, and in business anyone would be a complete fool to meet with you without their lawyer present also!'

'Did I say we would be discussing business?' he questioned. He listened to the sudden silence that clattered down the line at him, then added, *'Boa noite, amante,'* in husky dark Portuguese. *'Sonhos doas.'*

And he broke the connection.

Cristina stood taut, seething with anger and frustration—and fear. *That Goodnight, lover* had landed its message. The *Sweet dreams* had told her exactly what he expected her to go through for the rest of the night.

He was not going to give an inch. He had her hooked and he knew it. Just as he knew that the dreadful kiss in the white marble bathroom had ignited things inside her that were going to haunt her sleep. If she ever slept again, she thought with a shudder, when just thinking about that kiss drenched in her tight, stinging, sensual heat.

She did not want to want Luis again. She did not want to feel so out of control like this!

The knock at the bedroom door was hardly a warning before it swung open—just as she was about to do something stupid like throw herself down on the bed to weep her aching heart out. Gabriel stood there, big and strong, jacket and tie gone, amber eyes still brooding.

'You were lovers,' he announced, like an accusation.

She threw herself on Gabriel instead, landing with a sob against his wide, white-shirted front, and just cried her eyes out while he stood, maybe shocked but silently supportive, until it was over. Then he quietly sent her off to the bathroom to wash and change for bed. When she came back he had folded back the bedcovers. Without a single word passing between them he watched her lie down, then curl up like a defenceless child.

The covers were folded over her. Gabriel sat down on the edge of the bed. A gentle set of fingers reached out to brush her loosened hair from her cheek.

Her stupid eyes filled with yet more tears.

'It was there in the way you called him *Luis*,' he explained gently. 'And in the sexual tension that flashed like static around you both. But I stupidly did not realise it until a few minutes ago. When you ran he followed, like a man with a purpose—a sexual purpose—and earned you an enemy in his lovely companion.'

'Are *they* lovers?' The words shot right out of the sudden burn of acid jealousy clawing at her breast.

'Well, she certainly wants them to be,' Gabriel said dryly. 'And she did not like it when you snatched him literally right out of her grasp.'

'She can have him with my blessing.' And she meant it—she did!

'So tell me about it,' Gabriel invited.

Cristina closed her eyes and refused to speak—then was almost instantly flicking them open again. 'What do you think you are doing, Gabriel?' she demanded as she watched him heeling off his shoes.

'Getting more comfortable.' To her further consternation he stretched out on the bed beside her, then reached for her and drew her against him. 'Be calm,' he said lazily, when she went to push away. 'You are as safe here in my arms as you will ever be in a man's arms, and you know it. But I am not leaving here until you tell me everything. You understand me, Cristina? I want to know it all.'

'We had an affair six years ago.' The words left her reluctantly.

'Ah. Would this be the year of the mysteriously missing Cristina Marques?'

'I ran away,' she admitted. 'My father would not let me go to college, so I went without his permission.'

'And angered him greatly.'

'Do you think I cared about that?' A slender shoulder gave an indifferent shrug to her father's feelings. 'He believed a woman's place was in the home, playing slave to her men.' She did not add that he had also believed he had the right to marry her off to whoever would pay him a large injection of cash.

'He was a bullying tyrant.'

'*Sim,*' she agreed. 'I thought you were going to go out again?'

'My lover can survive without me for one night,' he said.

'This is much more interesting than sex. How many people would love to know what happened to the beautiful Marques heiress during the year she went missing?'

'Some heiress.' She laughed bitterly, thinking that the only thing she had inherited was the useless Marques pride, while Gabriel closed his eyes and envisaged his beautiful gold-skinned lover sulkily awaiting his arrival and understanding nothing.

'Continue, please,' he said. 'You ran away from home and went to college…?'

'No.' Cristina frowned. 'I had to earn the money to pay for college first, so I managed to find a job working in a bar on the Copacabana and slept in a little cupboard of a room on the floor above…'

It had been a hot and airless little room, and the hours she'd worked in the bar had been long. She had just begun to wonder if fate at her father's hands might not be better than what she had landed herself in, when Luis had strolled into the bar.

Tall, dark, handsome Luis, with the beautiful English accent and the sensational smile. Her heart gave a pained little throb, and, curling up against Gabriel, she told him everything—almost everything—from their instant attraction to each other to her moving into his apartment to live with him.

Her missing year had been a wonderful year, filled with love and passion and laughter, an introduction to the kind of world she had never believed really existed outside the pages of romantic books. His apartment on the Copacabana had been a haven in which they'd lost themselves.

'…then his *papa* died in a car accident and he had to go back to England,' she concluded.

'End of story?'

End of them, Cristina thought bleakly. '*Sim,*' she said.

'You simply waved this passionate lover farewell, then went back to Santa Rosa?'

That came three months later, Cristina remembered bleakly. 'We did not part—pleasantly,' was all she said out loud.

'He wanted you to go with him?'

No answer to that one.

'But you preferred to marry Vaasco Ordoniz instead?'

No answer to that one either. But he felt her fine shudder of revulsion when he mentioned her dead husband's name.

'And now your passionate ex-lover is back?'

'Sim.' She did answer that one. No use denying it. Luis was back. Bigger than she remembered him to be, leaner and harder, and colder than she remembered him to be, and so much more potently desirable than she remembered him to be—and the memories had been potent enough.

'He has offered to bail me out,' she admitted.

'And the price?'

Cristina moved restively. Sex was the price. Retribution was the price. Last time he had offered her marriage. This time she would be offered—something else. She could deal with *something else*. In fact, she was truly shocked and terrified by how much she wanted to have something else with Luis again.

'I will find that out tomorrow, when I meet with him.'

'You have already arranged this?'

'Sim.'

Gabriel sat up. 'And when were you going to get around to telling me of this meeting?' he demanded.

'I'm only just getting used to the idea for myself!'

He made a sound of impatience. 'You had better give me the time, so I can free myself up. I have a very busy schedule tomorrow, and if Senhor Scott-Lee is moving this quickly then we will—'

'No, Gabriel,' Cristina cut in softly, placing a hand on his arm. 'I want to thank you from the bottom of my heart for coming to my aid tonight, but from now on I will deal with this by myself.'

'Don't be foolish, Cristina.' He frowned down at her. 'The man is a shark beneath that smooth cloak of English sophistication. And he's hungry. I saw it in his eyes when he looked at you. He wants to eat you, *querida*. If he is about to offer you a rescue package then he means to play with you a little first.'

And he is powerful enough to play with you too, if I let him, she thought sadly. 'No,' she repeated. 'I know him. I can deal with him better if I do it by myself.'

CHAPTER FOUR

IT WAS all right to be brave, and determined to go it alone like this, but from the moment Cristina stepped into the hotel lift that would take her up to the top floor suite she knew that she wasn't feeling brave at all.

Gabriel was right. She had to be a complete fool to come here alone. She was just asking for trouble—begging for it.

The lift came to a stop. Her insides began to tingle, but what worried her most was that the tingle was not entirely to do with fear. As she stood facing the doors, waiting for them to open, those tingles went chasing down her arms and her legs in tight anticipation of—what?

Seeing Luis waiting for her dressed in one of those white bathrobes he'd always used to favour? Luis with his long tanned legs peppered with crisp black hair on show, and the triangle of hair that used to curl temptingly around the lapels of the robe?

An otherwise naked Luis. A man making a statement— a *You are here to please me or else* kind of statement.

Would he be that obvious, that crass, that—?

The doors began to move. Suddenly she lost the ability to breathe. Then her chin was lifting in the automatic response of a woman who'd learnt to meet trouble with defiance. If Luis was thinking he could march her into the nearest bed then he was going to have a—

A woman stood there. The same blonde woman Luis had been with the night before.

'Mrs Ordoniz?' she enquired in coldly cultured English,

giving no hint whatsoever that she had so much as set eyes on Cristina before in her life. 'I am Kinsella Lane, Mr Scott-Lee's personal secretary. If you will follow me, please, I will take you to him…'

No Luis to greet her personally—dressed or undressed. No threatening intimacy of a hotel suite with a bed very much on show. Just a private foyer, with several closed doors leading from it, and a woman who called herself Luis's personal secretary—but only a fool would believe that. Why else would she be here, in Luis's private suite? Did she share the accommodation with him? Did they share his bed as well as his suite?

Anger rose, fizzing on the edge of jealousy as she followed in Kinsella Lane's blue-suited wake. She knocked briefly on a door, then swung it inwards and was gliding forward on her long model's legs.

'Mrs Ordoniz to see you, Anton,' she announced in a low, intimate voice.

Several things struck Cristina hard at the same moment, the name *Anton* being the hardest strike, tugging her to a stop as the man himself came into view. He was leaning against the edge of a long conference table that spanned almost the full width of a room made up almost entirely of pale wood.

Two other men were with him. Cristina didn't see them. She only saw Luis, but not Luis, wearing a steel-grey business suit with a waistcoat that hugged his front like a piece of finely tooled armour worn over a bright white shirt and silver tie. His neat black hair, his golden features, even the long-fingered hands he used to add expression to whatever he was saying placed an aura around him that trapped the breath in her chest. And he was speaking in English, laying out instructions in clean, crisp, deep-bodied tones laced with authority that held his audience captive and mute.

This man was not the magical warm dark Luis she'd used to know. He was *Anton*, the ruthless banker, a gladiator of business, wearing the suit of armour of a man used to and comfortable with power in a way he had not been six years ago.

He turned his head to look at her then, and with the light coming in from a window behind him his eyes appeared even darker than hers. Two disturbingly black spaces set between slumbrous eyelashes that began lowering as he made a slow study of her from the neatly contained hair and conservative black suit to the unremarkable style of her low-heeled shoes.

She looked as if she'd come here to attend a funeral, Anton was thinking, and felt a wave of anger shoot through him, followed by a twinge of something else that he did not want to analyse.

He'd spent long enough analysing the grim state of Cristina's finances to know she owned hundreds of square miles of top-quality grazing land, thousands of heads of pedigree beef. She owned a whole mountain and a lush, fertile valley between it and a strip of rainforest that stood between the developers and a prime stretch of Atlantic coastline. But she'd had to borrow the money to make the flight to Rio.

It was no wonder she'd come here wearing unflattering black. The last time she'd worn that terrible suit had probably been to her wastrel of a father's funeral, and before that the funeral of her lousy gambler of a husband. Today had to feel like yet another funeral to her.

The death of the Marques pride.

That twinge tightened its grip on him. Pity? his mind suggested anyway. But what was there to pity about Cristina? She'd turned her back on him to marry for money.

For the thoroughbred continuance of the Marques blood-line. You didn't pity that, you derided it.

And where was the brood of pure-blood child stock?

Nowhere. Vaasco Ordoniz had died childless, and if anyone knew why then it had to be himself. So, no, he did not pity Cristina, he informed that uncomfortable twinge across his chest.

But he did still desire her—more so when she dared to lift that chin to him, as if to say *To hell with what you think of me. I am what I am and you will not change that.*

Well, that remained to be seen.

Kinsella demanded his attention then, by touching his arm and saying something softly to him. Forced to drag his eye away from Cristina, Anton found that his secretary was standing a bit too close. He said something curt—he didn't know what. Then he took a moment to dismiss all three employees while his attention fixed itself back on Cristina's defiant stance.

What he did not notice until the three shifted into motion was that the electric current running through the room was so strong it had removed the ability to breathe. His two young executives were curious. They'd never seen him this distracted by anything—especially by a woman they believed he was about to indulge in a perfectly ordinary business meeting with. Kinsella, on the other hand, had picked up on the sex sparking through the tension, and he noticed the hostile flash her blue eyes gave Cristina. That look alone told him that she was piqued.

If she did not watch out, his super-efficient secretary was going to have to take a move sideways, out of his orbit, he decided.

Then forgot all about Kinsella as the door closed behind her.

They were alone.

Silence fell.

Was her heart beating as rapidly as his? Was she standing so still because, like him, she was afraid that if she moved all this sexual static would ignite and explode in a glorious barrage of untamed want?

And those eyes...

Those wide-set, almond-shaped, luster-dark eyes were looking at him as if they would dearly love to put a curse on him but were too busy trying not to eat him alive.

The look hit him where he'd expected, hard between his legs, pouring those warm pleasurable hormones into his bloodstream as his sex began to swell. She'd done this to him the first time he'd ever set eyes on her, turning him back into a sex-charged schoolboy unable to control the urge. That she could still do it to him now, dressed as she was and looking at him as she was, should be surprising him. But, having spent the night before in a state of high arousal on her account, he'd had to come to terms with the unarguable fact that this woman did it for him all the time, like no other woman—still.

Then she did surprise him, breaking the tension gripping both of them by dragging her eyes away and moving across the room to stand staring out of one of the side windows at the view. It wasn't the same spectacular view he got from the windows in the private part of his suite, but then this was a conference room, and conference rooms were designed for business not to give people a riveting vista of Rio. Nor were rooms like this designed for seduction. But in his private suite—

He grimaced, deciding not to let his mind go there—yet.

'You could at least say *Hello, Luis*,' he prompted dryly.

'You are not Luis, you are Anton,' she coolly replied.

Another grimace worked its way across his mouth, because he knew exactly who he felt like.

Hell, he knew that.

'I suppose this means that you expect me to call you Senhora Ordoniz?' he countered.

She turned to look at him. 'I am a Marques,' she announced, in that proud way she had of saying that name. 'I always have been and I always will be a Marques. I never used the Ordoniz name, so I would therefore appreciate it if you would stop using it and inform that—Kinsella Lane person of this, so she will not make the same mistake again.'

Kinsella? A black satin eyebrow arched in curiosity. 'Jealous of her already?'

The taunt earned him a flash from her eyes. But she remembered as well as he did what a naturally jealous and possessive little witch she'd used to be.

'She is your paramour—don't bother to deny it.' She dismissed the way he opened his mouth to do just that. 'I saw it in her face when she looked at you. I heard it in that silly husky voice she used to speak to you when all I received from her was a chill.'

'Paramour?' Anton repeated. 'What an old-fashioned word to use.'

'Mistress, then.' It made no difference to Cristina.

'A mistress is reliant solely on the generosity of her benefactor for her pampered existence. Kinsella holds down a good job and relies on no man for anything—unlike some.'

He meant herself. Cristina stiffened. 'I was never your mistress.'

'I housed you, clothed you, fed you and bedded you— good definition of a mistress.' He shrugged.

She ignored that. 'Paramour suits her better—the way she flutters around you like some silly fluffy moth.'

'But she is so beautiful, and so very willing, *meu*

querida.' He smiled tauntingly. 'She also comes with no strings attached. How is a man supposed to resist?'

'Then enjoy her.' Cristina turned her face back to the window.

'The position is yours if you want it.'

'I don't want it.' She added a toss of her head.

'Then that,' he said, 'concludes our business.'

Unimpressed by the shocked face she swung round to show him, Anton levered his long frame upright from the desk, his mood swapping from teasing to deadly serious with a speed that took her by surprise.

'You know why you are here, Cristina,' he said grimly. 'If you are being foolish enough to let yourself think that you're in a position to bargain with me, try thinking it through again.'

'I will not share your bed with another woman!' she tossed at him tautly.

'You will do as you are damn well told!' he lanced back.

And it was there, just like that—his contempt for her, the cold anger that froze her where she stood.

Cristina pulled in a deep breath. 'I don't understand how you can want me when you feel such hate for me,' she said as she breathed out again.

'Strange, that.' He grimaced. 'I've been puzzled by the same thing myself. I hate you, but you can still turn me on faster than any other woman of my acquaintance—and that, *querida*, is your only bargaining chip,' he warned. 'So be sensible and use it to your advantage instead of questioning it. Now, come and sit down.'

He swung out one of the black leather club chairs that lined the length of the table, then calmly reached out to hook up a phone.

'Coffee, please, Kinsella,' he instructed. 'Brazilian, and make it strong…'

Cristina hadn't moved a muscle by the time he turned back to her. His eyes turned a darker shade of green. Tension leapt as he began striding towards her like a lean, sleek hunting cat. One glance at the set of his face and alarm bells were ringing, sending a shot of adrenalin shooting down her spine. She knew that smouldering expression—recognised it from the evening before. Sparks began flying. Sexual sparks. That dreaded familiar heat began to pool between her thighs. On a short breath of air she took a wary step backwards, met wall and window, and put out her hands.

'Anton—'

'Luis,' he corrected, bypassing her hands to coil long fingers around her elbows and used them to tug her against his chest. There was a moment's stifled stillness between them as his eyes held her eyes and then he lowered his head and claimed her mouth.

It wasn't a pleasant kiss, or even that deep a kiss, but still by the time he lifted his head again there wasn't much of her that wasn't quivering.

'Okay, we have a choice at this juncture,' he said coolly. 'We can attempt to behave like civilised people, and sit down over there to discuss our business. Or we can go in the other direction, through that door you can see over there…' he indicated '…which leads to the very private part of this apartment, find the nearest bed and conclude this side of our business first. Now, which is it to be? Your decision.'

Her decision? Cristina thought dizzily. She let the tip of her tongue trace the pulsing contours of her lips and stared fixedly at the knot of his tie while she tried to find the strength to speak.

His hands still had possession of her elbows; her hands lay splayed across his chest. She could feel the muscular tightness of his body beneath the fitted waistcoat, feel his heart pumping to an accelerated beat that was telling her which option he would prefer.

And she was tempted. It appalled her to realise just how much she was tempted to throw business to one side and just take the rest.

'Tough choice?' he prompted when she took too long to answer. 'Need a little help?'

Before she realised what he meant he'd lowered his head again, touching his lips to the corner of hers. A sigh feathered her throat as instinct sent her head turning in a hunting move to capture that mouth, but it had already moved on, brushing her flushed cheek to send a fine quiver of pleasure running through her when he found her earlobe and gently closed his teeth on the tender soft flesh. Her breath feathered again and she moved that bit closer, fingers shifting in a tense little movement upwards, to the wide spread of his shoulders, then compulsively into the silk dark hair at his nape.

The soft sound of his laughter barely registered as derision until he released her lobe and murmured, 'Business should always come before pleasure, *querida*, as any street hooker should know.'

It took a full second for it to sink in that he was likening her to a street hooker. Cristina tugged herself free. Humiliation surged up from the quivering mess her senses were in and, without saying a word, she stepped around him, walked on cotton wool legs to the chair he'd pulled out for her and sat down on it.

Behind her, she felt his cruel amusement reaching out to her. In front of her lay nothing but more glass, set too high in the wall for her to see anything but uninterrupted blue sky. Her eyes burned, her heart hurt, inside she could feel herself coming to pieces—sitting tensely on the part of her anatomy that was twisting and twirling with the heated excitement one kiss had fed into it while the rest of her crawled with self-loathing.

Because he was only telling it as it was. She *was* little more than a street hooker, here to sell the only commodity she had that he was interested in.

The silence between them throbbed like a struggling pulse-beat. If he said one more word to her Cristina knew she was going to further humiliate herself by breaking down to weep. Maybe he knew it. Maybe he still possessed enough sensitivity in his hardened soul to recognise it. Because all he did was take up his previous position against the table, dominating everything within her fixed vision, even the patch of blue sky. Crossing his long legs at the ankles and folding his arms across his chest, he waited in silence for her to calm down.

He'd shattered her, Anton could see that. Blank, hurt-blackened eyes were standing out on her pale face. The knowledge should be filling him with satisfaction but, oddly, it was doing the opposite. Six years ago she had shattered him, crucified everything he'd believed they felt for each other, then calmly walked away. If revenge for that moment had been his motive for doing this to her then he was discovering that he did not like what it made him feel.

Suppressing the urge to issue an apology, he moved his gaze to the contours of her mouth. It looked so tiny, held under control despite the evidence of his kiss still pumping blood into the lush lower lip. The delicate heart shape of its upper partner had a deeply vulnerable look to it that made him want to…

His eyes drifted lower as he imagined that beautiful skin stripped naked for him to see and touch. Was the rest of it still as smooth as her face was? Did her skin still shine like golden silk? He saw his hands drifting over her, felt the pleasure in stroking such perfection, then frowned as a different pair of hands took the place of his. Old hands, gnarled and withered hands, belonging to the man she had married in his place.

Anger leapt up inside him, growing on a wave of bitter, bloody disgust and contempt.

'Let's talk about your marriage,' he said abruptly.

She stiffened as if he'd shot her, and something flashed across her eyes—gone before he could catch it.

'My husband is dead,' she stated coldly. 'And I will not discuss him with you.'

'Not even to throw in my face how you married him within a month of turning me down?'

She sent him a silent icy stare in reply.

'Ordoniz left you destitute. So perhaps I can understand your desire to pretend he did not exist.'

No response again.

'And your own father was no better,' he continued. 'He squandered everything of any worth to that Marques pride you try so hard to hang onto. So take my advice and try not to say the name as if it should mean something of respect to me, because it doesn't. Okay?'

Okay… He was after her blood now, ruthlessly diminishing her to nothing in a few well-chosen statements.

'Do you feel better for saying all of that?' she asked stiffly.

'Hurt, did it?'

'*Sim.*' No use in pretending that it had not.

He nodded, but did not actually voice the *Good*. It hung there in the space between them all the same. He wanted payback for every cruel thing she had ever said or done to him. Making her swallow the truth about the Marques pride was only the beginning. There was, she was sure, much more to come.

'What does Enrique Ramirez mean to you?' he asked next.

Cristina almost shot from the chair in shock. Never in million years had she expected *that* name to come up in conversation with anyone! It took every bit of control she had in her to keep her voice level when she said, 'Enrique who?'

But Luis had noticed her first reaction. His eyes narrowed. Her skin began to crawl with heat.

'Ramirez,' he repeated, very dryly. 'A man of about your father's age—a good-looking guy when he was in his prime…' His mouth turned down as he said that. 'He was a favourite with the ladies…got rich by marrying diamonds and oil. Played polo for Brazil and was a bit of a celebrity here for a—'

'Polo?' Cristina looked up, her breathing fracturing.

'That means something to you?'

'M-my late h-husband used to train polo horses,' she told him, looking away again. 'It was a major part of his life until…'

Her world tilted into silence as a far-distant memory replayed itself in her head. She was seeing a small child, breaking free of her career to run towards the paddock, unseeing of the dangers—how could she see them? She was too young, and she loved horses. Scooting under the fence was the quickest way to get closer to them. She heard a horse galloping towards her, turned to face it, then froze. Wide-eyed, she watched it try to stop short of her, snorting and skidding and in the end rearing up high while its rider tried to stay on its back.

'Go on,' Luis prompted, unaware of what she was seeing in her head. 'Your husband trained polo horses until—?'

'H-he had an accident,' she breathed unsteadily. 'He was trampled beneath one of the horses and was badly injured. He never went near a horse again afterwards, but—'

Her world tilted again, turning her face quite white as she sat there, seeing Vaasco hitting the ground, then the lethal power of the horse's hooves pounding into him. The horse was confused, scared as it tried to disentangle itself. It reared up again, huge, like a great roaring giant to the small child, then came thundering down with—

Cristina leapt to her feet, gasping sharply—she just couldn't stop herself.

'What the hell—?' Luis was suddenly grasping her arms in support.

It took another shaky breath to pull herself together. 'I have remembered that I have heard that name before,' she breathed, lowering her eyes from him and fighting to keep the tremor out of her voice. 'Enrique Ramirez was the name of the man who pulled the horse away from Vaasco, at great risk to his own safety. I—V-Vaasco owed his life to him.'

'You added a *but* before you went as white as a sheet.'

'Did I?' The sheet-white face turned perfectly blank.

'Were you there, Cristina?' Luis questioned narrowly. 'Did you witness your husband's accident?'

An odd kind of smile touched her pale mouth. 'It happened years ago. I was only a very small child.'

'Your husband told you about it?'

'Oh, yes,' she replied, with strange bitter smile.

'And also mentioned Ramirez by name?'

'Why are you interested in Enrique Ramirez?' She threw in her own question.

'Nothing important.'

It could have been the imminent arrival of the ordered coffee that made him let go of her so abruptly, but somehow Cristina did not think so—because she might have been economical with the truth just now, but she had a suspicion that so had he been, with his 'nothing important' throw-away.

Then again, the way he'd moved away from her like that could have more to do with Kinsella Lane being the person carrying the coffee tray, she decided, as she watched him stride across the room to meet the other woman halfway.

The fact that Kinsella had picked up on the tense atmosphere was clear in the look she sent Cristina before she carefully lowered her gaze.

Anton had seen the look also, and frowned as he reached out to take the tray.

'A Senhor Pirez has called several times to speak to you,' Kinsella informed him stiffly.

'No calls,' he instructed as the tray changed hands.

'Senhor Pirez was very insistent.'

'And you know the drill, Kinsella,' he responded. 'When I say no calls, I mean no calls.'

Cristina watched the other woman's blue eyes glint beneath her lashes before she turned and walked stiffly out of the room. Clearly she did not like his censure.

Had they had a lovers' spat? she thought nastily. But that was how she felt—nasty and mean and bitter and—

'You should be careful. She knows why you have brought me here,' Cristina heard herself snipe as he walked towards her with the tray.

'Meaning?'

'She is dangerous, that one. You think I was a jealous cat, but she will scratch your eyes out if you dare to take another woman to your bed.'

'Whereas you will grin and bear it for the sake of the money I can offer you.'

'I have told you once.' Cristina's chin came up. 'I do not share a man's bed with other women.'

'What about another man?'

The question confused her. She frowned at him and he smiled as he placed a cup in her hand.

'Gabriel Valentim,' he enlightened her. 'Did you share his bed last night?'

She was tempted to lie and say *Yes—passionately*, but there were already too many lies between them. 'I am not involved with Gabriel,' she said coolly.

'Lover without the loving?' He took a sip from his cup.

'Gabriel is just a friend.' She took a sip of coffee too.

'*Just* a friend?'

'A long-standing friend,' she extended. 'His father has been our family lawyer for ever. It is just your nasty mind that wants to make our relationship more intimate than that.'

'He's a good-looking guy. He's reasonably well-heeled. You need money.' A lazy shrug of a wide shoulder said the rest.

'Not as rich as you,' she hit back. 'And he is also *gay*,' she added, 'So you will please keep your unwanted thoughts to yourself.'

Gay.

Anton stared at her for a moment, then threw back his dark head and laughed. He'd spent the whole of last night lying wide awake in his bed, tormenting himself with visions of the handsome swine locked in Cristina's eager arms, when all the time—

'I don't know what you find so amusing in hearing that.'

'I don't suppose you do,' he replied, still smiling as he rid himself of his cup.

Cristina did the same at that exact moment, and their arms brushed. It was like making contact with a live wire.

Sparks shot through his body, then gathered at his loins. Anton sat back very slowly. Cristina simply froze. It was getting worse. Maybe the bed option before the business one was the right way to go, he considered wryly.

Cristina pulled in a deep breath. What was the matter with her? Why was she feeling like this? For six years she had kept all her emotions firmly under wraps. Then Luis walked back into her life and suddenly she was finding she could not control anything.

'Anton—' she burst out. 'Can we—?'

'Small hint, *querida*,' he interrupted. 'When the only thing you've got going for you is the intimacy of a name, then use it. Anton is a ruthless bastard. You really do need to keep him out of this as much as you possibly can.'

'And who is Luis? Anton's nice, *kind* alter ego?'

'His *sexual* ego,' he enlightened her. 'Luis is sitting here aching to strip you naked and sink himself so deep inside you he will never find his way out. Anton aches to see you stripped of everything but the clothes on your back.'

'A no-win situation, then.' She sank back into the chair in a helpless gesture.

'That depends on what you want out of this.'

I want you to look at me with those eyes lighting with the flames of love like they used to, Cristina thought helplessly.

'Your help,' was what she said. 'I want you to help me save my home.'

'That's it?'

Pressing her lips together, she nodded.

'At any price?'

'Almost any price,' she modified, with a nervous touch of her tongue to her suddenly dry upper lip.

He said nothing for so long that Cristina was forced into looking at him. He was staring at her mouth. Her heart gave a thump; lips he'd brutally kissed not that many minutes ago began to reheat. She wanted to look away but she couldn't. She wanted him to say something but he still didn't speak. The heavily laden silence began to weave around her like a silken web. He was so beautiful, her Luis. So—

'Okay.' He nodded. 'Then let us see if we can find the ceiling on your *almost any price*.'

Hooking out another chair from beneath the table, he lowered his long frame into it. 'This is how things stand for you, Cristina, and it isn't good,' he warned. 'The Alagoas Consortium have decided to fight dirty. They are in the process of trying to buy your mortgages, plus all the other debts you've managed to incur. If they succeed they will turf you out of Santa Rosa without giving you a chance to catch your breath.'

'You said you would help.'

'But on my terms, *querida*. And non-negotiable terms at that.'

The *almost* test. She could hear it coming. 'What kind of terms?' she asked huskily.

'A large stake in Santa Rosa.'

Cristina nodded, having expected to hear him say that.

'Full control over how the money I invest is spent.'

That brought her chin up. 'You know nothing about farming!'

Green eyes glinted. 'But my future wife does.'

Future *wife*—? It had not occurred to her that he might be getting married! Jolted into a reaction, she felt her backbone tense and jumped to her feet.

'You will not bring another woman into Santa Rosa, Luis!' she spat at him angrily. 'I would rather take my chances with the Alagoas Consortium than let you!'

His hand closing around her wrist silenced her. 'Your

tantrums used to turn me on, Cristina. Now they do not. You are badly used goods, *querida*, wearing a badly used suit which makes you even less appealing. So try at the very least to find a little dignity. Sit down again and listen,' he instructed icily.

Cristina sat, slaughtered by his brutal opinion of her. Letting go of her wrist, Anton sat back.

'Now, this is what happens,' he continued, as if the incident in the middle had not taken place. 'My bank will buy you out of trouble. It will keep Santa Rosa ticking over until such time as you fulfil your part of the deal.'

'Which is what?' she asked bitterly.

There was a pause—a carefully constructed pause that held Cristina completely trapped. Then it came—smoothly, calmly, quietly.

'I need a wife,' he announced. 'And I need one quickly. You, *meu querida* are in the fortunate position of suiting my requirements.'

CHAPTER FIVE

SHEER disbelief had Cristina twisting to stare at him. 'You are asking *me* to marry you?' The words arrived gasping from her lips.

Anton's face hardened, his whole demeanour turning to ice. 'Take note, Cristina, that at no point in this discussion am I *asking* you to marry me,' he said, very clearly. 'This is a business arrangement. I need a wife,' he repeated. 'You happen to fit the bill. You are young, presentable, and still desirable.'

'Even for badly used goods?' she quavered.

'As you say.' He nodded. 'You also need my money *more* than I need you.'

'*Why* do you need a wife?'

'That's my business.'

'You want a *silent* wife?' She was unable to stop the slicing sarcasm from coming out.

'You could say that—though I think it might be stretching my luck.' He smiled in spite of the ice.

'I wonder you are not putting your secretary in the role, then.'

'She does not suit my requirements.'

'But she would not say no to you.'

'Are you thinking of saying no to me?'

Cristina was too busy trying to grapple with it all to say anything.

'Maybe you would rather let Kinsella suffer my English touch than be forced to suffer it for yourself again.'

That did it. She turned on him, swivelling in the chair to

69

burn him with a look. 'I *never* once said I did not enjoy making love with you, Luis!' she said hotly. 'And stop throwing my six-year-old words back at me!'

'Strong words, though, Cristina. Hard words from a proud Marques mouth.'

'As you have already pointed out, what pride is there now in being a Marques?' she countered, then had to heave in a deep, unsteady breath. 'The name, like my reputation, is demolished. Do you think I am too stupid and too *proud* to have realised that for myself, long before you came back into my life?'

'My apologies,' he said.

She looked away from him and said nothing. An apology only meant something if it carried regret.

'Am I allowed to ask what my role as *wife* to you is supposed to entail?'

'Of course you may ask,' he answered, so smoothly it was like a slap in her face. He was sitting there—*relaxing* there now—as if the anger of before had never been, while she…

Was hurt and fighting not to show it.

And afraid of what was going to come next.

'Your role will be the same as any other wife,' he told her. 'You will keep my house, be my hostess and sleep in my bed. You will also make yourself available to me for sex whenever I desire it…' He sat forward then, so he could look into her face. 'And here is the bad one, Christina, so prepare for it because you are not going to like this,' he warned. 'We—as in you and I—are going to have to go all-out for a fast and probably furious attempt at conceiving a baby. I need you to be pregnant, you see, within a few months…'

Having shot his final past-avenging dart into her useless little heart, Anton watched, totally riveted—because it actually was like witnessing a murder take place. She seemed to die right there in front of his eyes.

'Too much to ask?' he prompted.

She didn't answer.

'Still protecting your gorgeous figure at all costs?'

She still made no response.

Something vicious tightened inside him. 'Or perhaps you still cannot face the prospect of my half-English blood mixing with your blood?'

She breathed then—blinked. One of those very slow lowerings of fine-veined eyelids over terrible blank eyes. As they lifted again so did Cristina, rising out of the chair like a zombie. Then she just turned and walked towards the door, leaving Anton sitting there, stunned and so damn angry that she could do this to him—again!

He threw himself to his feet. 'I see that we have found your ceiling price,' he fed harshly after her. 'But know this, Cristina. The deal remains in place only until you reach that door!'

She stopped walking, trembling from hair root to toe tip.

'I *hate* you, Luis,' she whispered painfully.

'I am so gutted by that, *querida*,' he drawled in return. 'Do you go or do you stay?'

She spun on him then, her beautiful face blanched of its warm golden colour, dark eyes shot through with a kind of agony that had him folding his arms across the sudden tightness trying to band his chest.

'Stay for what?' she cried out shrilly. 'So that you can take more revenge for that precious ego that I bruised so badly once?'

'Did you bruise it? I don't remember.'

'I battered it!' she spat at him. 'I crushed it in my fist and flung it to the ground! You want more of the same from me, *querido*? You want to feel the same rejection again?'

'Reject me, then. Use the door,' he invited. 'You never know—if you spread your net wide enough you might catch another withered old man willing to buy his way into that sensational body of yours.'

She flew at him then. It did not surprise him. He'd been goading her towards it since she'd first walked through the door. The tied hair, the grim suit—as a disguise they were useless where he was concerned. With every flash of her eyes and every smart-mouthed comment he'd seen the real Cristina lurking there. Now she was out, and he was going to make sure that she stayed out.

He fielded her arrival without having to do very much other than catch her as she arrived at his chest, wrap his arms around her and lift her clean off the ground. Their faces came level—hers whitened by stark fury, his as un-giving as rock. She hit out at him with her fists. He laughed—once—harshly, then treated her angry mouth to a totally carnal flat-tongued lick.

All hell broke loose with that one action. She quivered from wetted lips to slender thighs. A whimper broke from her—a sobbing, cursing protest. He did it again, only this time he took the lick inwards and turned it into a full-blown deep and devouring assault. Her angry protest vibrated through both of them. As he levered himself away from the table and started walking her fingers clawed into his hair.

Did those fingers attempt to pull his mouth away from her mouth? Not this woman. She held him down, held him right there, where she was greedy for him. He knew her. He knew what made her explode sexually—and what made her *his*!

When he reached the door that would give them access to his private suite, he flattened her against it with his body, so he could use his hand to seek out the handle. As the door swung open, with the weight of their bodies as impetus, he had to use his hands against the heavy wood to cushion the moment when it hit the wall behind and they followed it. Her feet found solid ground again, but she didn't let go of him. So they remained there, pressed against the door, kissing like hungry maniacs for long lost minutes. Time in which he managed to rid her of her jacket. The skirt was too big. He had only to release the zip for it to fall in a heavy whisper to the floor.

Did she let go then? Did she come to her senses? Did she even *know* this wasn't six years ago? Not this hot, greedy, sexually hungry woman who pushed his jacket from his shoulders with impatient fingers and sent it dropping to the floor with her own clothes.

Her hair came next, pins flying as he loosened that glorious mass of twisting ebony and let it tumble over his fingers. She was working free the buttons on his waistcoat when he lifted her up again. She wrapped her legs tightly around his waist, took his bottom lip between her teeth and bit.

It hurt. She had meant it to. When he winced out a curse she did it again. When he attempted to pull his head back she imprisoned it in her hands, then she was the one to instigate the next mouth and tongue-devouring kiss.

She was wild for him. He loved it. Exhilaration ran through him as he made the move to the bedroom by pure instinct. She clung. He pulsed. She moved against him. His hands gripped her bottom and she felt like satin, warm, too slender, too delicate to be real. He dropped her on the bed, then came down with her, the heat of need pounding through his body and scoring streaks across his hard taut cheeks.

His mouth ached, his jaw, his warring tongue. He broke

the kiss to look down at her and watched as she gasped and panted for air.

'Are you staying or going?' he demanded in a voice as cold as an English winter. The stark contrast between his physical self and his mental self was so acute that she stared at him for a full ten seconds before reality finally sank in.

'You want your pound of flesh!'

'I want more than that,' he responded. 'I want your thankless little soul gift-wrapped and handed to me with a rock-solid guarantee that this time it belongs to me!'

Cristina looked into the hard, cold, face of this man she loved so much and had hurt so much, and wished there was a tiny molecule of hope for them.

But there wasn't. 'You will come to regret it,' she told him honestly.

'Are you staying?'

'You will learn to hate me all over again.'

'You are not here because I adore you, *querida*. You are here because I still want you.'

It should hurt to hear him say that, but it didn't. How could it hurt when she did not deserve more than he was offering?

'In your bed?' She demanded confirmation.

'Yes.'

'As your obedient little sex slave?'

His green eyes began to gleam. 'Most certainly that.'

A strange smile touched the corners of her hot pulsing mouth. 'Gift-wrapped?'

'*Sim.*' He swapped languages so there could be no mistaking the answer.

'You can have me like that without marrying me.'

'I had you like that once before. Didn't like it. So the marriage thing stays. It comes with the package.'

As the baby did? She wanted to weep all over him—but she didn't.

'The gift-wrapping?' she asked.

'The rock-solid guarantee of a marriage certificate—written in blood if need be. I will not compromise,' he warned huskily.

Take it or leave it. Take this man when you know that you should not. Take everything he wants to dish out to you in the name of revenge when you know you will end up having to walk away.

Again.

Eventually.

'So, are you staying?'

She made no answer, her beautiful eyes so painfully, hauntingly bleak that something too close to fear grabbed at the muscles in Anton's chest. He did not want to be hooked by her again. He wanted Cristina firmly hooked by him.

'Answer or leave,' he ground out roughly.

She looped an arm around his neck and drew his mouth back down to hers.

Was it an answer?

He was going to take it as one. Choice was something ripped away from him the moment her tongue made a sliding caress over the top of his. She lifted a long silken leg to loop it around his hips in one of her old, uninhibitedly sensuous and possessive moves, and on a surrendering growl he let himself fall prey to the whole wild experience that was Cristina Marques, the enemy of his once bitten ten times shy heart.

Mouths open, hot and fused. Her fingers back at his waistcoat. She all but ripped it from his body, setting the tight satin muscles in his shoulders rippling as she tugged it down his arms. His tie came next—an impatient yank at the slender knot and silver silk slithered apart—and she was already opening the buttons on his shirt. Eager, needy, her fingers made familiar contact with the whorls of dark hair covering his thundering breastplate, curling, then scoring into his flesh to make him shudder with pleasure as he brought his own impatient fingers to the hem of the cotton T-shirt she wore.

They had to break the kiss so he could strip the T-shirt over her head. Separation brought with it a moment of sanity as he felt the thinness of the fabric. Well washed and well-worn, he saw, and made a mental note to buy her a new wardrobe as he tossed the scrap of cotton aside.

Then he saw them. Proud, unfettered, full and firm. Two golden globes tipped by long dark nipples standing up in bold and brazen demand. On a growl he pounced, sending her slender spine arching on a high-pitched quivering cry as he took possession in an open-mouthed, wet-tongued, hungry claim.

His shirt hung open. Her fingers crawled all over hard muscle and taut male flesh. When he sucked, she writhed beneath him, and he ground out a soft curse as electric sensation shot to his thighs. As if she knew, she located the fastener for his trousers and began an urgent attempt to strip him of those.

It was no use. He was forced to help because there was no way she was going to succeed while he still wore his socks and shoes. Sitting up with a growl of impatience, he reached down to remove the obstructing articles while her hands slid beneath his shirt and began a sensual exploration of his satin-smooth back.

His shoes hit the floor, followed by his socks, then he stood up to remove the trousers. She watched him, her eyes like burning rubies, coveting each new piece of hard male flesh he revealed.

No other woman had ever looked at him the way Cristina looked at him.

'Greedy,' he muttered as she reached out to touch him, brushing feather light worshipping fingers along his full length. He throbbed and swelled and hardened so fast it was almost an agony. He had to fight with uncoordinated fingers to release cufflinks so he could remove his shirt.

Stripped naked he was beautiful. *'Bonito,'* Cristina murmured.

Still beautiful…*always* beautiful. Her Luis, she thought helplessly as she drifted her eyes over his tall dark stance, with its arrogant masculine pride in his own prowess.

He came down beside her, stretching out along her slender length, then sliding an arm beneath her shoulders and lifting her towards him. He held her like that, with her hair rippling behind her and her passionate mouth parted, ready for the hungry onslaught of his.

Eyes like glowing emeralds looked deep into her eyes. He didn't speak. She didn't want him to. If he did they would fight, and all she wanted to do was make love. Would he know, afterwards, that he had been her only lover ever? Could men tell these things?

He moved then, claiming her mouth with a hot, deep, probing assault that pressed her back against the pillows so he could cover her with his warm naked weight. After that it was a voyage of rediscovery, hot and intense and achingly poignant. Neither bothered to look for restraint.

And six years was a long time to starve a fever. It was hungry and it wanted feeding. They fed it. Oh, yes, they fed it. The rest of the world might have come to an end and they would not have noticed or cared.

Neither heard the quiet footsteps making their way across the living room. Neither recalled that they'd left the doors to the conference room and bedroom hanging wide open.

Kinsella Lane stood in the bedroom doorway. She had been there for a long time, watching like a voyeur and listening to everything they said, with the cold blue eyes of hate.

She wanted Anton. She had always wanted him, from the moment she'd first seen him when she was only a very junior secretary at the Scott-Lee Bank, much too low in the ranks for him to notice her. She'd worked long and hard to gain entry into his select circle. She'd made a careful study of all the different women who'd floated in and out of his life. He liked blondes. She'd become a blonde. He liked them slender and neat, supremely elegant and sophisticated. She'd learnt how to achieve that elegance and sophistication. She'd honed and pruned and sculpted herself to meet the specifics of his sexual criteria. And he had begun to notice her. She'd seen the warmth grow in his eyes when he looked at her—felt the telling sting of his attraction towards her begin to catch light.

When he'd brought her along on this trip to Rio she'd thought it was because he was ready to deepen their relationship. His rejection of her in the lift the other day had hurt. But then two other employees had been present, so she'd understood and learnt yet another lesson—get your timing right. Or so she'd thought.

Now look at him, locked in the arms of the complete opposite from everything he had ever been attracted to. She was dark, she was small; she wore ugly clothes. Her hair was a mass of wild black twists and her breasts were too big. And there was no sophistication in the way she kissed him or touched him or taunted him or even spoke to him. Yet he was mad for her!

It was there in the way he shuddered when she caressed him. No finesse. No smooth, slick seduction. Just animal hunger and hard, hot sexual feast. Even the way he was covering her now and reaching round to wrap her legs around him showed an animal with no grace.

His lean golden flanks rippled as he made that first lunging thrust into her body. Her cry of pleasure echoed round the room.

Turning away in disgust, Kinsella left as silently as she had entered, stepping over discarded clothes and touching nothing, not even bothering to close those doors.

As soon as she gained the privacy of her office she opened the safe and took out the file Anton had placed there that morning, after his private meeting with a man called Sanchiz. Ten minutes later and she was replacing the folder in the safe, then picking up the telephone and dialling London.

'Mrs Scott-Lee?' she said. 'I think you should know that your son is intending to marry a Brazilian woman. A young widow—Cristina Ordoniz.'

There was a long silence, then a faint, slightly tremulous question. 'Ordoniz, you say? Are you sure of that name?'

'Yes,' Kinsella confirmed.

'And young, you said? How young?'

'About my own age, Mrs Scott-Lee,' Kinsella answered. 'I understand that her husband was an old man when she married him for his fortune. Not quite the person you'd want as a wife for your son, I would think.'

Anton's mother made no response to that. And there was another one of those silences before she said, 'I will be catching the next flight to Rio. Thank you for helping me with this, Miss Lane…'

He'd forgotten what it was like to have her breathe his name all over him. Forgotten too much, Anton realised as she blew six years of other women to absolute Hades and

rolled him up, tied him up and packaged him with a label—
Belonging to Cristina Marques.

Did he care? The hell he cared, he thought as he made
that first driving thrust inside her, then stopped, watching
in dark eyed fascination as she tensed, then cried out in an
echoing response to their first time together, when she'd
given him her virginity without bothering to warn him that
it was there.

'Long time, *querida*?' he questioned huskily.

'*Sim,*' came the gasping reply.

Her fingernails were scoring deep grooves into his shoulders, and the slender arch of her body was an instinctive
attempt to fight off his invasion. For a short, frowning second he thought of withdrawing, but she opened her eyes
and looked directly into his.

Her mouth shook, but she said, 'Don't you dare, Luis.'

He smiled then, amused by how well she too was remembering that first time, when he had tried to withdraw
only to have her stop him. And, like that first time, he
reached up to brush her hair from her face, then lowered
his mouth to gently soothe her with soft kisses while he
waited for the tension to ease.

Familiarity should breed contempt, but not in this case.
Familiarity was everything when she lifted up her hands to
cup his face, then began whispering soft words of love
against his lips. In one way he did not want to hear them
spoken; in another way he lapped them up with true macho
arrogance as she told him everything she was feeling, everything she wanted to feel, and eventually, as the tension
eased from her body, everything she demanded he give.

And he gave it all. He gave everything. They matched.
They'd always matched—in hunger, in passion, in what
they wanted and demanded and made sure they received.
They kissed, they touched, they rolled, they built it. It was

hot and it was fevered. Each surging thrust overpowered the previous one; each coiled-spring meeting of their bodies drove them closer to the edge. He kissed her mouth, her breasts, her fingers when they came back to his face. When he felt the first ripples of her growing climax he lost it completely and quickened the pace. She came as she'd always come—wildly, noisily, gasping and shuddering and tugging him with her over the edge.

Afterwards they lay in a heap of tangled limbs and sweat-slicked skin and shuddering senses. He could feel the thunder of her heartbeat and the quiver of her lips against his throat.

'Well, that was worth the six-year wait,' he murmured eventually.

'Don't talk,' she said, and he grimaced.

Maybe she was right. Talking was bound to spoil everything. Rolling onto his back, he took her with him so she lay along his length with their bodies still joined and no desire on either side to separate.

Her hair was stuck to his face and he reached up to brush it away, then gently rearranged her into a more comfortable position, with her cheek in the damp, cushioning crook of his shoulder and her boneless legs resting along the sides of his.

He was sated, he realised, then thought, Strange, that. Because the feeling had nothing to do with the sex but with this—having Cristina lying on top of him like a warm, sleek, sleepy cat.

Reaching for one of her hands, he lifted it to his mouth and began idly tasting each slender finger while he attempted to work out why he was feeling like this.

Cristina, on the other hand, was trying to work out how she'd break it to him that marriage was out of the question, no matter what slant he wanted to put on what they had just done.

Why did he need a wife, anyway?

Or a baby?

The thought of the latter addition made her start to tense up. He instantly soothed her with the featherlight brush of his fingers down the length of her spine.

Luis was always like this after making love, she remembered. Wide awake, but relaxed, content to keep her this close. Any minute now he would start to instigate a second loving. She knew it because she could feel him inside her, still a bold, probing force, even though he was not quite fully erect. And this time it would be slow, more deeply intense and sensually exploring.

Did she let it happen? Did she give in and steal just one more escape from reality before she told him that his deal was not going to happen?

'You told me you still love me,' he remarked idly.

'I did not!' she denied, lifting her head up from his shoulder so that she could glare that denial into his impassive face.

He was so beautiful her heart turned over. His slumbrous eyelids lowered as he sucked her index finger into his mouth and wrapped his tongue right around it, then began a slow mimic of a different act that set him hardening and swelling inside her.

Her soft gasping quiver had him releasing the finger.

'You did,' he insisted, then reached up and brought her mouth down on his before she could answer. A few seconds later and she had forgotten what they were talking about as it all began again in a slow deep mutual loving—just as she had predicted.

Just this one more time, Cristina told herself as she let him take her over.

*   *   *

Back in London, Maria Ferreira Scott-Lee was standing by her dressing table. In her hand she held a small package from Estes & Associates, Advocates of Law, Rio de Janeiro. The package had arrived the same day that her son had flown out to Brazil. Inside it was a jewel box and a letter. The jewel box held an exquisite, priceless diamond-encrusted emerald ring. The letter was personal—deeply personal—handwritten by Enrique himself.

Don't mess with what you do not yet understand, Maria, Enrique had written as a warning footnote. *Our son will marry the widow of Vaasco Ordoniz and you will forget that you ever knew that name if you value our son's love for you.*

But she could not forget Vaasco Ordoniz. She could not forget that Anton would have been Vaasco's son if Enrique had not got in the way.

Ah, the tangles life could throw at you, she thought on a sigh that had her lowering herself onto the dressing stool. Enrique was the most handsome man she had ever encountered. Meeting him at Vaasco's ranch had turned into the ruin of her life. Betrothed to Vaasco, in love with Vaasco, she had still fallen for Enrique's charm and into his bed. When she'd fallen pregnant with Enrique's child she'd had to tell Vaasco. It was natural that he'd thrown her out of his life.

'Back to the gutter where you belong,' he'd said.

Sebastian had come to her rescue. It had been Sebastian who flew her back to Rio and eventually brought her to England with him. Dear Sebastian, who had been in Brazil to buy horses from Vaasco. He'd come back with a broken-hearted, shamed and pregnant woman instead.

Now here was life making a tangling full circle, and the

Ordoniz name was haunting her again. Who was this woman? How did Enrique know about her? Why had he sent their son to her? Who was playing a game with whom?

She was young, Kinsella Lane said. Vaasco had been a very wealthy man. He had trained horses for the polo field as a hobby, not to earn a living. Who was this—person who would marry an old man if she was not some kind of cynical fortune-hunter? And, having managed to inherit Vaasco's money, was she looking to get her hands on Anton's money as well?

Maria looked down at the ring box sitting on her dressing table, then at the words in Enrique's note.

For you, Maria, in sincerest gratitude for the son you gave me and as a token of my regret for the life you had taken away from you on my account. Our son grew in my image. He deserves to know this. He deserves his share in my inheritance. Vaasco turned out badly. One day you will perhaps thank me for saving you from him. Think on that when you meet his widow. She is not what she seems and deserves your pity.

'I pity no one who means to hurt my son,' she murmured.

Maria's son wasn't hurting. He was sleeping the sleep of the thoroughly sated.

Lying beside him, Cristina watched him—just watched, as she'd used to love watching Luis sleep. He had a way of sprawling on his front across three-quarters of the bed, leaving her one quarter to curl herself into. She never minded. When he awoke, her quarter would become his quarter too, leaving the rest of the bed to grow cool.

Or it would if she intended to be here when he awoke.

She had already delayed her departure for much longer than she should have.

But for now—for a few more precious seconds—she was content to reacquaint herself with the way his hair flopped over his forehead and how his face wore the relaxed expression of sleep.

Her tummy muscles quivered, her heart squeezing out a tight, painful ache. He was beautiful, her Luis. Passionate, demanding, insatiable—and the low-down pulse of just how insatiable still played its pleasure across the sensitive muscles where she loved to feel Luis most.

How had she lived six years without being with him?

How was she going to manage without him all over again?

They'd got up at one point between bouts of wild passion, gathering up clothes and closing doors. It had made her blush and him grin when they realised how they had left them standing wide open for anyone to come in and catch them.

'My staff know better than to intrude on my privacy,' he had stated with arrogant confidence.

Still, they'd been—noisy. She was blushing again now just remembering some of the gasps and cries she'd emitted in the throes of her pleasure. Or those tense little curses he'd rasped out as his control snapped, and the resulting driving sound of his breathing when he finally gave in.

He was no silent lover, this cool-headed half-Englishman she loved so much, Cristina thought with a smile. The desire to reach out and gently stroke that floppy lock of hair away from his forehead almost got the better of her.

But it was time for her to get up and go…

Stay a little longer, urged a soft voice inside her. See out the rest of the day, then the long dark night with him. Leave tomorrow.

No. The time to go was now…while she could.

Her heart gave that painful little squeeze in protest. At the same moment a pair of ink-black eyelashes lifted upwards and eyes the colour of a dark ocean focused on her face. It was as if he'd sensed what she was thinking, the way a set of long fingers reached up to brush a gentle caress across her cheek.

'You're still here,' he said softly. 'I was dreaming you'd left me.'

'No,' she whispered

Tomorrow, Cristina thought. I will leave tomorrow. 'Kiss me, Luis,' she begged.

CHAPTER SIX

IT WAS into the afternoon by the time Cristina let herself into Gabriel's apartment.

'Where have you been?' Gabriel demanded, almost before she had managed to close the door. 'It was bad enough that the rushed message you left with my answering service last night said almost nothing, but did you have to go missing today too?'

Having spent most of the day trawling through the banks and financial houses of Rio, it was all she could do to utter a weary, 'Sorry.'

'Not good enough, Cristina,' Gabriel censured. 'I was worried about you. When I rang Scott-Lee to find out what was going on, all I got was some cold Englishwoman claiming that she had never heard of Cristina Marques!'

The lovely Kinsella, Cristina thought dryly. 'I was there,' she said, then explained about the mix-up in names.

Gabriel shoved his hands into his trouser pockets. 'I was beginning to think he'd abducted you,' he said gruffly. 'I had this image of him bundling you into a sack and shoving you in the boot of his car, then driving off to some unknown location to have his evil way with you.'

'Not very English of him, Gabriel,' she mocked, though Luis had bundled her into bed pretty effectively, she allowed.

'He does not look very English...just sounds it.'

He makes love in English, Cristina thought, then had to turn away before Gabriel could see the look in her eyes.

Too late, though. 'You look like death, *querida*,' he observed gruffly.

Feel it too, Cristina thought. 'I need a shower,' she said, and walked down the hall towards her allotted bedroom.

Gabriel followed. 'You want to explain why you look like death?'

Not particularly, Cristina thought as she crossed the bedroom to open a drawer that held the bits of underwear she'd brought with her.

'I spent the day visiting the banks,' she told him, shifting to the wardrobe to rifle through the few items of clothing she had. Just two good dresses worthy of the kind of social events like the gala last night—both black. Vaasco had only allowed her to wear black.

'Scott-Lee's offer was not good enough?'

Her shoulders ached with the strain of trying to appear normal. 'It was not the right one.'

'As in…?'

As in I would be his willing mistress for the next fifty years even if he married another woman and had twenty children with her. But that was not what Luis wanted.

'He wanted your body,' Gabriel derived from her silence. 'Since you spent the night with him, I conclude that he *had* your body?'

A strained laugh escaped past the lump in her throat.

'I cannot believe that you were stupid enough to give him his reward before he'd handed over the money, Cristina,' he muttered.

It was so like advice for a street hooker that she swung on him angrily. 'Don't speak to me like that, Gabriel!'

But he was angry too. 'What did he do? Seduce you with a load of promises, take what he wanted, then throw you out on the street this morning?'

No, I sneaked away when he wasn't looking, Cristina

thought heavily. 'Can we leave the lecture until after my shower, please?' she requested.

'Sure,' Gabriel replied, and stormed out, leaving Cristina to wilt down onto the end of the bed, recalling how she had left Luis.

She'd pretended to be perfectly content to lie curled in his bed while he got dressed for a business meeting at his bank. She'd even smiled when he'd kissed her farewell and let that kiss cling enough to send him away with a rueful smile upon his face. The moment he'd left the suite she'd been out of that bed and racing for the shower.

Coward, she thought now. Weak little coward.

It was probably appropriate that she should have met Kinsella Lane in the hotel lobby, wanting to come into the lift as she was leaving it. The blonde had taken one look at her and said, 'Bitch,' shocking a neatly dressed young man standing to one side of the lifts. When she'd tried to walk away Kinsella had grabbed her wrist and spat the kind of venom at her that was still turning her stomach. 'Don't kid yourself that I will stand back and let you take my lover away from me, because I won't. It was my body he drowned in the night before you fell into bed with him, and it will be me he will return to London with.'

Odd how the truth had the power to hurt so much, Cristina thought now. Because Luis *would* be returning to London with Kinsella, and she—

She spied her suitcase, sitting at the bottom of the wardrobe, and on a sudden burst of urgency pulled it out and tossed it onto the bed. She did not want to think about what she would be doing when Luis returned to London. She did not want to think of anything other than packing her case and catching the first flight to Sao Paulo she could get a seat on, and to hell with—

The door swung open. Gabriel stood there. Big and lean

and endearingly handsome, even with that look of contrition on his face. 'I did not mean to insult you,' he apologised gruffly.

'I know that.' And, strangely enough, she did. Gabriel had been her friend for too long for her to take any real offence because he gave it to her as he saw it.

'I was worried about you.'

'*Sim.*' She understood that too.

'I was concerned that you were desperate enough to snatch at any rescue package placed on the table if it stopped the Alagoas Consortium from raping your land.'

'You know what, Gabriel?' Her shoulders sagged suddenly. 'I thought so too…'

'But it did not work out like that?'

No, it didn't. Luis had found her ceiling price without even knowing it.

'I'm going home,' she said quietly.

'Since I am watching you pack, *minha amiga*, I have managed to make that assumption,' Gabriel drawled. 'But then what will you do?'

The answer to that was frighteningly simple. 'I don't know.'

And neither, by his silence, did Gabriel.

'Get your shower,' he advised, after one of those dull, throbbing moments. 'I will see if I can get you a seat on a flight to Sao Paulo tonight.'

The shower went part-way to lifting her flagging spirits, aided by her refusal to let herself think. She spent time blow-drying some of the wetness from her hair, then left it to do its own thing while she applied a light layer of make-up, then put on fresh underwear, followed by the jeans and a white T-shirt. All she had left to do was to finish packing.

Placing the case ready by the front door, she made her way along the hall towards the kitchen, following the aroma of freshly made coffee. Pushing open the door was the simple part. Taking in the sight that met her eyes was not simple at all.

Her heart ceased to beat, robbing her of the ability to do anything other than stand there and stare at the two men casually propping up the kitchen units, drinking coffee like old friends. Both were wearing dark business suits, their jackets hanging carelessly open over white shirts and dark ties as they sipped coffee from white porcelain mugs. Only one of them had the power to hold her so thoroughly trapped like this.

'Luis…' She breathed his name.

'Does she always call you Luis?' Gabriel asked curiously.

'Unique to Cristina,' Anton replied, eyes like green granite as he flicked them over her loose hair and her casual T-shirt and jeans.

'W-what are you doing here?' she demanded stupidly.

'Treading in the shadow of your stubborn path.' A black eyebrow arched. 'Did you really expect me not to come after you?'

'Cristina has always been stubborn,' Gabriel put in conversationally. 'You have an English saying I cannot quite bring to mind that describes this stubbornness perfectly…'

'Cutting off her nose to spite her beautiful face?'

'Ah, *sim.*' Gabriel nodded. 'She also hates to admit it when she is wrong…'

Dragging her gaze away from one man, Cristina looked at the other. It did not take many brain cells to read the message in Gabriel's tone. While she had been showering he and Luis had talked. Gabriel now knew that the rescue package was not only rock-solid but that it came with a very respectable offer of marriage as well. The dream solution, in other words, for not only did she get the money she needed to save Santa Rosa from the wicked developers, she got herself a good looking, filthy rich husband willing to save her miserable, empty little soul at the same time!

Cristina pulled in a breath. Her chin went up. 'I see,' she said as she breathed out again. 'From hating each other, the two of you have now become firm allies over a friendly cup of coffee. Well, forgive me if I don't bother to join you.'

With that she turned and walked out—*escaped* was a more honest word. Inside she was trembling and shaking, shocked to find Luis here and truly afraid of what it was going to mean. She'd seen the anger burning in the green granite. She'd heard the warning threat threading his smooth silken voice. And even as she hurried down the hall towards her suitcase she knew she was running scared.

The hand that reached for her suitcase before she could pick it up told her everything. The strong arm that became a manacle around her middle said a whole lot more.

'Packed already?' Luis said lightly. 'Good. Then we can leave.'

'I am not going with you,' she told him, standing like a wooden plank in the crook of his arm.

'You are,' he returned without compromise. 'We made a deal.'

'I changed my mind.'

'Before or after the sex?'

'Before,' she declared. 'I took the sex because it came free.'

'You think?'

'I know.'

'Nothing comes free in this world, sweetheart,' Anton mocked. 'So, say thank you nicely to Gabriel, for letting you stay with him, and then set your treacherous little backside moving out of the front door or I will throw you over my shoulder and carry you out!'

Cristina heaved in a hot breath as she twisted round in his grasp with the intention of fighting herself free. Only it didn't work out that way. His arm banded her closer, and she found herself inhaling the clean, washed smell of him, and the much more disturbing scent of very angry male. Looking up into his face, she caught the flare of green in his eyes just before she heard her case hit the ground. Then his other hand was taking control of her nape, and all she managed was a husky, quavering, 'Don't...' before she received the full force of his mouth on hers in a punishing, plundering act of pure vengeance that left her shocked, shaken and shamefully desperate for more.

Feeling like a boneless quivering wreck, it was all she could do to subside weakly against him, her face pressed into his shirt front while he held her there and talked over the top of her head to Gabriel as if the kiss had been nothing at all.

Just the fact that Gabriel had witnessed it was a further humiliation she had to contend with. When she heard him say, 'I will leave the small print to you, Anton,' Cristina felt as if she'd lost her only friend in the world.

Anton retrieved her case and pushed her towards the door. She went quietly after that. The lift took them downwards. Neither spoke. A chauffeur driven black Mercedes waited at the kerb. The moment they were both encased in its plush leather interior the car moved off. She sat staring out of the window. He sat staring directly ahead. He was angry...she was angry.

'I suppose you told Gabriel that I am the love of your life?' she said tightly.

'I told him what he needed to hear to let you walk away with me.'

'Lies.'

He released a dry laugh. 'You fell apart in my arms over one short kiss, so don't blame him for believing what his own eyes could see,' he charged. 'And we are both good at lying, Cristina, so you can drop that reproof from your voice. It cuts no ice with me.'

'Does anything?' She sighed.

'No.'

'Gabriel—'

'Is no fool,' he incised. 'He knows I make a better friend than I would an enemy. Let him believe he allowed you to come with me because it's what you really want. It's safer for him.'

She turned her head to look at him then. 'You are so powerful these days?'

He didn't even bother to look at her. 'Yes,' he said.

He made her shiver. He made her truly fear the man he had become.

'Leave Gabriel alone,' she whispered.

'If you possessed a modicum of sense, *querida*, you would be worrying about your own situation more than your friend.'

He turned his head to look at her for the first time since they'd left Gabriel's apartment then, and Cristina's heart gave a wary little squeeze in her breast when she looked at him. Everything about him was hard, coldly angry, intimidating.

'I don't know where you get the arrogance to think you can play games with me a second time,' he delivered coldly.

'I was not playing a game,' Cristina replied. 'I just needed—'

'The sex,' he cut in. 'So you thought, Why not get it from Luis since he's so damn good at it?'

Her cheeks flushed. 'We did not have sex, we made love,' she corrected.

The expression of derision in his eyes as they glinted at her made her want to crawl away inside her own skin and hide. She knew on one level that she deserved his anger. She knew that in the way she had sneaked out of his suite while he slept she had taken the coward's way out. But—

'You were bullying me, Luis!' she hit back accusingly. 'You backed me into a corner and gave me no room to think! I left because I needed some time to consider what you were proposing!'

'I'm sorry to tell you this, *querida*, but you don't have the luxury of time or choice.'

Something landed on her lap. Cristina stared down at it for several long seconds before reluctantly picking it up. By the time she'd finished scanning the sheets of legal jargon tears were clogging up her throat.

'When did you acquire these?' she asked in a stifled whisper.

'Before I stepped foot in Brazil,' he replied. 'As you can see, *I* own you, Cristina. Not various banks and loan companies. I own the power to decide what happens to your precious Santa Rosa. And if I decide to foreclose on your debts and sell out to the Alagoas Consortium, I can promise you that it will happen—the very next time you attempt to walk out on me.'

It was such a brutal, totally unequivocal statement of intent that she shuddered. Luis owned her. He all but owned Santa Rosa by taking on the never ending length of her debts—the bottom line total of which, when laid out in black and white, actually made her feel ill.

They arrived at his hotel. Anton got out of the car and came around to her door, then took hold of her hand and pulled her out.

She came without protest, and it was crazy but that annoyed the hell out of him. He didn't want her beaten and subdued. He wanted her out here fighting—because when she was fighting he could fight back.

And he wanted to fight with her. He wanted to build it and build it until it progressed to a different kind of fight. She was in his blood again, like a fever. The sexual fever that was. Cristina Marques.

His hand trailed her into the hotel foyer. The concierge saw them enter and attempted to catch Anton's eye but he pretended not to notice. He did not want to talk to anyone, be pleasant or polite. He made directly for the bank of lifts, cursed silently when they were forced to share it with a pair of young lovers who couldn't keep their hands off each other. They laughed and teased and touched and kissed all the way up to the floor below his own. Standing rigid beside him, Cristina stared unblinkingly at the lift console. He stared grimly at the floor.

The moment they reached the privacy of his hotel suite Cristina twisted her hand free and walked away from him. Anton made for the bedroom to deposit her suitcase. When he came back she was standing in the middle of the room, staring at an empty wall.

His chest made that tightening clutch at him. Grimly ignoring it, he crossed to the drinks cabinet.

'Why?' she fed unsteadily after him.

He did not attempt to misunderstand the question. 'Call it payback for six years ago,' he answered. 'You owe me for six years. For my inability to believe what any other woman says to me—for not daring to believe what my own senses are telling me about them.'

'I never meant to do that to you.'

He swung round. 'Then what did you intend?'

Exactly what she had achieved, Cristina thought bleakly,

PLAY THE
Lucky Key Game

and you can get

Do You Have the LUCKY KEY?

FREE BOOKS
and a FREE GIFT!

Scratch the gold areas with a coin. Then check below to see the books and gift you can get!

YES!
I have scratched off the gold areas. Please send me the **2 FREE BOOKS** and **GIFT** for which I qualify. I understand I am under no obligation to purchase any books, as explained on the back of this card.

306 HDL D7ZE   106 HDL D72F

FIRST NAME   LAST NAME

ADDRESS

APT.#   CITY

STATE/PROV.   ZIP/POSTAL CODE

2 free books plus a free gift   1 free book

2 free books   Try Again!

Offer limited to one per household and not valid to current Harlequin Presents® subscribers. All orders subject to approval. Credit or Debit balances in a customer's account(s) may be offset by any other outstanding balance owed by or to the customer.

www.eHarlequin.com

DETACH AND MAIL CARD TODAY!

© 2002 HARLEQUIN ENTERPRISES LTD. ® and ™ are trademarks owned and used by the trademark owner and/or its licensee. (H-P-10/05)

The Harlequin Reader Service® — Here's how it works:

Accepting your 2 free books and gift places you under no obligation to buy anything. You may keep the books and gift and return the shipping statement marked "cancel." If you do not cancel, about a month later we'll send you 6 additional books and bill you just $3.80 each in the U.S., or $4.47 each in Canada, plus 25¢ shipping & handling per book and applicable taxes if any.* That's the complete price and — compared to cover prices of $4.50 each in the U.S. and $5.25 each in Canada — it's quite a bargain! You may cancel at any time, but if you choose to continue, every month we'll send you 6 more books, which you may either purchase at the discount price or return to us and cancel your subscription.

*Terms and prices subject to change without notice. Sales tax applicable in N.Y. Canadian residents will be charged applicable provincial taxes and GST.

If offer card is missing write to: The Harlequin Reader Service, 3010 Walden Ave., P.O. Box 1867, Buffalo, NY 14240-1867

BUSINESS REPLY MAIL

FIRST-CLASS MAIL   PERMIT NO. 717-003   BUFFALO, NY

POSTAGE WILL BE PAID BY ADDRESSEE

HARLEQUIN READER SERVICE
3010 WALDEN AVE
PO BOX 1867
BUFFALO NY 14240-9952

NO POSTAGE
NECESSARY
IF MAILED
IN THE
UNITED STATES

which had been to make him hate her enough to leave her and never come back.

Only he had come back, and now here he stood—hard, coldly angry, still hating her for which she had done to him. Though now the hate had sexual desire to feed his determination to carry this through to its bitter end.

'So all of this is for revenge,' she murmured emptily.

Glass in hand, Anton offered a shrug. 'And to solve the immediate problem I have that demands I get married and produce a child.'

Those words cut so deep that Cristina actually quivered, dark pain clouding her eyes. 'Then you have chosen the wrong woman for this—quest you are bent on,' she told him, and had to pull in a breath to steady herself before she could go on. 'B-because I cannot give you that child, Luis. I am not able to—'

It was like watching ice explode. The way his face altered as he slammed down the glass and then made a grab for her set her whimpering in surprised shock.

'Don't *ever* utter that lie to me again—understand me?' he rasped down at her.

Cristina lifted her pale face. 'It was not a lie—'

'You lie every time you open that lush red kissable mouth!' he bit out. 'You lied six years ago when you told me you loved me, then enjoyed watching me squirm as you put that particular lie to death!'

'No!' she cried brokenly. 'It wasn't like that! It—'

'It was exactly like that!'

Meu Dues, Cristina closed her eyes—because he was right, it had been just like that. 'If you will just listen to me for a moment, I can explain—'

'You know what?' He unclipped his fingers from her shoulders. 'I don't want you to explain. Your reasons no longer interest me. You owe me. I'm collecting—on my terms.'

He turned back to his drink.

'Terms I cannot deliver.'

He twisted round again. 'My terms,' he repeated hardly. 'As in you as my wife, my willing sex slave and the mother of my child.' He spelled it out yet again. 'In return you get your precious Santa Rosa, gift-wrapped, with all debts cleared. Fair exchange, in my view.'

'Or a choice that is no choice,' she murmured indistinctly.

'Which means…?'

Which means… She was feeling so very cold now that she had to wrap her arms around herself. 'I will marry you,' she said.

There was a single second of total silence. A long, sharp needlepoint second when he stared at her as though he could not believe she had surrendered at last.

Then, 'Say it again,' he instructed. 'And this time say it much clearer, so there can be no more misunderstanding. Because this is it, Cristina. Your last chance. I am not playing any more games here. So say it loud and clear so I know that you mean it.'

'You will regret it,' she whispered.

'Say it,' he repeated.

'All right!' she flashed at him, and in true Cristina style she rose to her surrender with the proud lift of her chin. Silky black hair went spiralling back from her narrow shoulders, her eyes flashing his coldly ruthless and unremitting face a look of burning contempt.

'I will hate you, Luis, for treating me like this and making me behave like a whore,' she told him. 'I hate you already, for your threats and your blackmail and your thirst for revenge that makes you want to treat me this way. But

I *will* marry you,' she repeated clearly, as instructed. 'I will sell myself to you like a whore in the marketplace in exchange for Santa Rosa—and when you discover how empty your revenge cup will be I will stand like this in front of you and laugh in your face!'

Luis moved without warning. She was trembling and panting so badly by the time she had finished that she just didn't see him coming, and before she knew it she was somehow plastered to his front.

Her stomach flipped. 'No,' she protested.

'Say that again in thirty seconds,' he challenged, and delivered his mouth to hers with a lip-crushing deep-tongued kiss.

Cristina did not need those thirty seconds. She did not need even ten to reduce to such a melting, boneless mass of quivering compliance that she couldn't think of anything else. She was useless, lost, his eager plaything. Her mouth clung to his mouth; her fingers clung to his head.

Then it stopped. Why it stopped she had no comprehension. It took more seconds than it had taken her to sink into it to float back out of it again.

'Great way to hate, *querida*,' his husky voice taunted. 'It excites the hell out of me, anyway…'

It was like being smashed when he'd already broken her. On a pained little whimper she pulled herself free and ran for the bedroom.

Anton winced as the door landed in its housing. He spun around and snatched up his drink, downed it, then went to pour another one—only to stop himself when he realised what he was doing, and stare grimly into the bottom of his empty glass instead.

He'd got what he wanted from her, so why wasn't he feeling better about it? Why was he standing here feeling as if he'd just lost something vital instead?

Her face. It had been the look on her face when she'd finally accepted there was no other way out for her. She called it hate; he called it—pain.

Why pain? He slammed the empty glass down, because he suddenly remembered that he had seen that look once before—six years ago, when she'd sliced him to pieces with her rejection. Had the scorn she'd used to do it been masking pain then, only he had been too blind to see it?

Oh, stop looking for excuses for her, he told himself angrily. He did not understand her. Thinking about it, he never had understood what really made Cristina tick.

What was it about her that she could make out that she despised him with all she had in her, yet fall apart in his arms without much of a sign that she had any control over what she did?

The buzz words were Santa Rosa, he reminded himself. Not him. Not the sex. Santa Rosa.

The bedroom door suddenly flew open. Cristina was standing there like a wild thing. He felt his body respond with enough heat to set him on fire.

'You can tell that manic secretary that your affair with her is over!' she tossed at him.

'You are in no position to bargain,' he threw back. 'Just think of Santa Rosa and I'm sure you will get over her presence in my life.'

The door slammed shut again. On a tight curse Anton turned and poured himself that second drink. Then he laughed—he *laughed*!

God, there was no other person alive on this earth who could arouse him to just about every emotion going.

He put down the glass because he discovered that he suddenly did not need the whisky. Still trying to control the smile, he headed for the conference room instead, where a full day's business awaited his attention. Where the hell he had got the idea that he could come to Brazil and play the hotshot banker *and* deal with Cristina he would never know.

While Anton was trying his best to lose himself in business matters, in a very sedate, very upmarket office in another part of Rio, an old man with white hair and immaculate grooming sat carefully filing his nails while he listened to the report being relayed to him by an unassuming young man with the unassuming name of José Paranhos.

Until now Senhor Javier Estes had been quietly satisfied with the information being relayed to him. All, it seemed, was going to plan. Senhor Scott-Lee had taken up the challenge, and the object of that challenge was making it difficult enough to keep him dancing on his toes. He'd even smiled when he heard that Cristina had spent the night with Scott-Lee in his suite.

It was the next part that lost Senhor Estes his smile and sharpened his attention. 'Say that again?' He prompted confirmation. 'This woman accosted Senhorita Marques as she was exiting the elevator?'

José nodded. 'Senhorita Lane was very angry and very unpleasant,' the younger man expressed. 'She claimed that she and Senhor Scott-Lee are lovers and that they had slept together only the night before. Naturally, Senhorita Marques was upset.' He went on to relay what else the secretary had thrown at Cristina.

Frowning now, Senhor Estes dropped the nail file to pick up his pen and scrawl a few terse notes on the file open in front of him. The indication that those few notes represented a black mark against Anton showed in the way with which the words were underscored.

'*Obrigado*, José. You will maintain your observation and keep me informed.'

With a nod, José left the office, and Senhor Estes withdrew a sealed envelope from the file. The envelope was addressed to Cristina Ordoniz.

Cats set among pigeons, Javier mused, invariably caused mayhem…

CHAPTER SEVEN

LUIS was sitting at the conference table, attempting to concentrate on the information being fed to him. His two executives kept looking at him oddly when they constantly had to repeat themselves. He didn't blame them for the odd looks. He felt odd, enlivened and distracted, too damn sexually aware that Cristina was on the other side of that door over there.

The telephone by his elbow began to ring. Remembering that Kinsella was not in the outer office to intercept all calls because he'd sent her to the bank to pick up some documents, he reached out and picked up the phone.

'Scott-Lee,' he announced himself briskly.

'At last!' Maximilian rasped down the line at him. 'Where the hell have you been, Anton? I've been trying to contact you all damn day!'

Tensing up at the urgency in his uncle's voice, Luis flicked a quick frowning dismissal at the two other men. 'Why? What's wrong, Max? Has something happened to my mother?'

'You could say that,' the older man answered dryly. 'She's on her way to Rio,' he warned his nephew. 'Should be setting down at the airport as we speak.'

'Coming here? What for?'

'To put a stop to this crazy marriage you are planning, of course. What else?'

His marriage? 'How the hell did she find out about it so quickly?' he demanded incredulously.

'Far be it from me to want to put a spoke in Maria's

103

plans, Anton—I adore that woman like she was my own sister, *and* I have no wish to see you throw yourself away on some gold-digging widow—but—'

Anton stiffened like a board. 'Watch your mouth, Max,' he warned thinly.

'You mean this woman is *not* the widow of Vaasco Ordoniz?'

Anton did not answer that. Something else far more disturbing had grabbed his attention. 'You know Vaasco Ordoniz,' he declared in a driven undertone. It had been right there in Max's tone.

'I'm not getting into that one,' Max refused. 'That's up to your mother.'

His *mother* knew Cristina's late husband?

'But I will tell you this,' Max continued. 'There is something going on within the ranks of your team that quite frankly stinks. And, love Maria though I do, I refuse to stand back and watch while you are stitched up by some jumped up little secretary who is paid to keep her mouth shut about your movements, not ring up your mother with all the gory details. I mean, how can a man have a private life if some—?'

'What are you talking about, Max?' Anton thrust furiously into this bewildering tirade.

There was a moment's silence while his uncle absorbed that fury. Then he said, very seriously. 'Kinsella Lane rang your mother yesterday to inform her of your intention to marry the Ordoniz widow. Your mother reacted like a demented chicken and caught the next flight she could get on to Rio.'

Anton swore soundly.

'Maria has taken a suite on the floor below yours, Anton. And the very helpful Miss Lane arranged it.'

Kinsella had done all this behind his back? Anton was stunned and shattered.

'I've been ringing you on and off all day, trying to warn you about this—did the secretary tell you? I bet she didn't. I can read the tone of a machinating woman from thousands of miles away, and that one is dangerous. Do yourself a big favour and get rid of her. She's a risk to your security.'

Anton eventually put down the phone on a string of tight curses. His mind was whirling at the flood of information his uncle had just fed into it. Kinsella had been passing on personal information about him to his own mother of all people? How had she got that information? Nobody attached to his entourage knew anything about his plans to marry Cristina! *How* had she heard, seen, picked up anything? Unless—

He remembered the file from his investigator, which he'd placed in the safe yesterday. Kinsella had been irritating the hell out of him since they'd arrived here in Rio, and Cristina had accused him of keeping Kinsella around as a lover within minutes of clapping eyes on her. He'd flicked the remarks away as unimportant when any man with sense knew he should never dismiss the uncanny power of the female instinct when it sensed a rival in its presence.

Had his not very private secretary been snooping where she should not look? Found out all she needed to know about Cristina and then calmly called up his mother to relay the information to her?

His mother.

His mind flipped to the next pending crisis. Reaching out, he snatched up the phone to ring down to Reception and find out the expected time of arrival of Maria Scott-Lee. The inner curses became progressively more colourful as that conversation was concluded.

Then he pulled himself together and stood for a few

minutes, grimly sorting his priorities into some kind of order. By the time he'd done that he'd turned into the ice man.

As Cristina was the first to see.

He entered the bedroom like a bullet, strode up to where she was standing, staring out of the window, caught hold of her hand before she barely had a chance to turn round, and just hauled her out of the suite.

'What do you think you are doing?' she demanded as he tugged her inside the lift.

Swinging her into the far corner, he pinned her there with a hand pressed against the wall at either side of her startled face.

'Why did you marry him?' he delivered.

Cristina blinked, taken aback by the question. Then her eyes hooded over. 'I have told you before. I will not discuss that with you.'

'Why not?'

Folding her arms across her front, she stared down at her shoes and pinned her lips shut.

'He was wealthy when you met him,' Anton persisted. 'He only started gambling the money away after you came into his life. Could the gambling have had something to do with the fact that you conveniently failed to give him a son?'

Cristina went as white as a sheet, but still refused to react in any other way.

He moved in closer. 'Was the need to keep your gorgeous figure perfect worth what it cost you in the end, Cristina? When you finished up a poor widow who had to go back begging to her miserable father? Did *he* hold it against you that you had not produced a male grandson for him to leave Santa Rosa to? Or was that always your goal?' he pushed on relentlessly. 'Was the only way you could own your beloved Santa Rosa by making sure you would never produce a son?

'Well, I've got news for you,' he continued, when she still said nothing. 'You will have *my* child whether or not you want it. Son or daughter. I have no preference. And Santa Rosa will be placed in trust for that child to inherit, because it will give me such pleasure to watch you lose the one thing that you covet the most!'

He kissed her then, using his hand in her hair to tug up her face and laying the kiss on her like a brand of hate. Tears were sparkling in her eyes by the time he straightened, her burning mouth working on the desire to just break down and weep. Luis looked at her as if he would love to strangle her right here in the lift—but the doors opened and he was grabbing her hand instead.

The lobby was busy. People everywhere—standing, sitting, moving about, checking out or checking in. Cristina blinked the hurt tears from her eyes and looked up at the hard-as-nails profile of this man she knew she would never forgive for saying what he just had.

And she would never forgive herself for giving him reason to say it.

'Where are we going?' she asked unsteadily.

'Shopping,' he answered.

Shopping... For a few short seconds the meaning of the word just refused to register in her bemused head. Then it did register. Luis had just destroyed her and now he was walking her into the swish shopping mall attached to the hotel as if it was perfectly acceptable to knock her down then take her on a shopping trip.

Cristina bit her teeth together and said nothing.

Anton was wishing he could take back what he'd said in the lift.

But he was angry—still angry—about many things. Not

least the amount of interference and manipulation that was taking place in his life. Ramirez, his mother, Kinsella—he could go right back to the day of his birth!

And that crack by his uncle Max about his mother knowing Vaasco Ordoniz was niggling the hell out of him. It was just one more thing other people had knowledge about and he did not. If he had any sense he would just drop this whole crusade, go back to England and—

It was then that it happened. As if Ramirez himself was listening in on his angry thoughts, Anton came smack up against a heart-leaping thump that stopped him dead in his tracks.

He was standing in front of a jeweller's window. Tall, dark hair, Latin profile, and a way of resting his hands in his pockets that was so familiar it completely locked Anton up where he stood.

Was it? Could it be? What if it was? The desire to go over there and ask the man outright if he'd heard of Enrique Ramirez vibrated like an engine in his blood.

'Luis…?' Cristina prompted warily.

He barely heard her. He could barely hear his own thoughts above the humming going on in his head. The man turned, as if drawn by the mental energy he was generating. The moment Anton looked into his face he knew he was looking at a perfect stranger. No green eyes, no cleft chin— no hint anywhere on that solid-shaped face that he could reflect back to himself. The rushing sinking feeling shot through him.

'Luis, you're hurting my hand…'

He looked down at the woman beside him. Saw the expression in her face and relaxed his grip. His half-brothers—his *half-brothers*, he repeated, and felt his mind swoop into full focus on his main goal in all of this.

Whatever it took, he told himself fiercely. Money, blackmail, seduction—threats. This woman, who was looking up at him through rich, dark, warily questioning eyes, was going to be his wife as soon as he could make it happen. She was going to grow ripe with his child. And to achieve those two aims he was prepared brush aside anything and anyone that attempted to run interference.

In fact he was more than ready to run some interference of his own.

And it began right here, in the first shop he pulled her into.

An hour later and they were standing in the spare bedroom surrounded by designer bags containing the designer clothes that he had chosen because she would not.

'Put on the red dress,' he instructed. 'You have—' he glanced at his watch '—about an hour and a half.'

With that dictatorial announcement he strode out of the bedroom and closed the door, leaving Cristina to sink down onto the end of the bed, where she sat staring at the array of bags spread around her. Even with the confused mixture of anger, hate and total bewilderment she was feeling, there was a tiny dark corner of her that wanted to dive with a shriek of delight into the lot.

There were bags containing sensuous floaty skirts and filmy tops by Nina Ricci, evening dresses from Valentino, day suits from Armani and Chanel. She could see the Gucci logo, Prada, Jimmy Choo... In a short, breathtaking hour Luis had trailed her through a wonderland of purchases without once letting go of her hand. He'd perused, selected and thrown casually at hovering assistants. If Cristina had not responded when he'd asked for her opinion, he'd used their clasped hands to lift up her chin, then kissed her full on the mouth.

He'd charmed, he'd smiled, he'd tossed off light, teasing comments. The assistants had been starry-eyed with hero-worship by the time he paid his account—while she must have looked like a spoiled and petulant over-indulged lover by the frozen look on her face.

But those starry-eyed assistants did not know what was going on behind the charm he ladled out for their benefit. They could not know that those smiling green eyes were laced with anger, or that the kisses he laid on her lips were hard and cold with contempt.

Luis, she had realised very quickly, was functioning to his own agenda. Be nice to the future wife in public, but treat her like dirt beneath your feet when not.

His real agenda had been fed to his mother via the telephone, while Cristina sat miserably on the end of the bed. Yes, he was surprised to hear she'd arrived in Rio. The concierge had told him, of course—who else? No, he did not have time to share a pot of tea with her, but dinner would be nice. Eight o'clock in the Mezzanine restaurant? He was sorry he would not be able to collect her from her suite, but he had some business to attend to first, so would it be all right if they met in the lounge bar?

Kinsella arrived back from the bank looking her usual smooth, immaculate self in a cream roll-neck sweater that skimmed her figure and a pencil-slim skirt to match. Anton watched through hooded eyes as she moved around the conference room, clearing away the day's business. Cool and calm, super-efficient—not a single hair or carefully curled eyelash out of place. There was no way from looking at her that anyone would know the danger that lurked beneath that efficient façade.

'Join me for dinner tonight,' he invited, in a low, soft, husky tone of voice, and saw her catch her breath before she turned to offer him a carefully composed smile.

'I...' She went for female hesitation.

'My mother has just arrived from England,' he added. 'I thought we could turn her first dinner here into a special night.'

'And Mrs Ordoniz?'

He did not correct the name. 'Let's leave her out of this for now, shall we?' he suggested, with just enough intimacy to make Kinsella blush.

He could turn them on without batting an eyelash. Anton had always known he could do it, but would never have believed himself capable of using the gift so cynically.

'Dinner would be lovely…thank you,' she accepted.

She thought she'd got her man in her pocket at last.

She thought she had an ally in his mother.

She thought she was about to break into the inner circle of his close family, consolidate the two and end up with happy-ever-after. Having had his eyes opened wide by Max, Anton was seeing everything with such crystal clarity it actually shook him cold.

The dress was most definitely red, Cristina dryly confirmed as she followed its smooth and sensuous lines, cut to mould every curve she possessed and show off her long slender legs. The fact that she had not tried on a single one of Luis's purchases in the shop said a lot about his unfailing eye for size and style. The dress had long sleeves that began at her wrists and hugged like a second skin all the way up to the under-curve of her arms, leaving her smooth shoulders bare. And the bodice shot straight across her chest, just low enough to show a shadowy cleavage and the gentle slopes of her breasts.

Sexy, she thought as she viewed herself in the long mirror. Definitely very thought-provoking, without revealing too much naked flesh. Her mother's fake diamonds sparkled at her ears and her throat, and she'd put her hair up because she knew that Luis would not like to see it like that. But then she'd gone for compromise by teasing a few glossy twists free to fall around her neck and her face. Her make-up was heavy—the dress seemed to demand it—dark and sultry shaded eyelids, a double lick of black mascara on her curling eyelashes and of course a matching red lipstick that enhanced the passionate shape of her mouth.

And because it was a long time—more than six years—since she'd worn anything so openly gorgeous and sexy, she could not resist striking a flirty come-and-get-me pose and adding a lush-lipped pout.

'Now, that is the woman called Cristina Marques,' a deep voice murmured in appreciation.

On a soft gasp Cristina spun around so quickly that she almost fell off her new backless high stiletto shoes, a hectic blush mounting her cheeks at being caught girlishly playing up to the mirror.

Luis was leaning in the bedroom doorway looking everything he was in a black dinner suit and bright white dress shirt. All long lean lines of laid-back sartorial elegance, with that ever-present tummy-tingling underlying vibration of latent, purring, sexual male.

'I was beginning to think she had been banished for ever,' he went on in the same low lazy attitude. 'But here she is, beautiful and exotic in her new fine feathers, vivacious and sexy and loving it.'

The last two razor-tipped words pinned his mood. He was still angry. Cristina's chin came up, challenging, defiant. If her hair had been loose it would have been flying back from her shoulders.

'Even *viuva de* Ordoniz can enjoy dressing up on occasion,' she retaliated.

The relaxed lines of his face hardened. 'You claim never to have used that name. Don't use it now.'

Straightening away from the door, he moved across the room with the grace of a prowling panther. Arriving a short foot away from her, he came to a stop, overwhelming her with his height and his masculine presence, fluttering her heart muscles and turning her knees weak when she did not want to feel like that.

Reaching up to flick a fingertip at the diamond droplet dangling from her ear, he then hooked the same finger beneath the matching necklace she wore at her throat.

'Diamonds?' he murmured.

Opening her mouth to tell him they were paste, her pride stopped her—what bit she had left after the way he had been scraping her clean of such a vice.

'They were my mother's,' was all she said.

'Ah,' was all he said, and he gently withdrew the finger, leaving her to wonder if he would have ripped them from her if she'd told him that Vaasco had given them to her.

'I don't want to fight with you, Luis,' she heard herself say in a husky whisper, and wished she knew why she did.

'Who's fighting?' he said, dipping his hand into his jacket pocket.

Cristina shivered out a sigh. 'What happened between us six years ago was—'

'Six years ago,' he inserted. 'Forget it, Cristina. It is what's going to happen in the future that counts now.'

But for her the past and the future were as indelibly linked as night following day. 'You cannot—'

'I can do anything I like while I'm in the driver's seat.'

'Will you let me speak one full sentence before you interrupt?' she flashed.

'Not right now.' His hand came out of his pocket. 'Give me your left hand...'

She sucked in a tense breath. 'What for?'

'Just give...'

He took possession of the hand without bothering to wait for her to yield it. Cool fingers with a thumb pressing lightly against her palm dragged her eyes downward. It did not occur to her that he meant anything ground-shaking by the gesture. Even when he stroked a light touch across the base of her ring finger she still did not catch on.

'No mark,' he observed.

'No.' The mark that Vaasco's wedding ring had placed there had long gone.

'Good,' he murmured. 'I like that…'

It was then that she saw it, catching a fleeting glimpse just before the ring slid smoothly into place. Bright flickering diamonds clustered around a burning dark ruby set on a band of gold. Her heart ceased to beat, her throat closing over the thick lump that formed in her throat.

'Do you like it?'

Of course she liked it—she loved it! 'But—Luis…' She drew in a deep breath. 'We have to talk about—'

'Try to think of it as my stamp of pending ownership,' he described. 'Soon a wedding ring will have joined it.'

'Soon?' She looked up questioningly.

'Yes, soon,' he repeated. 'As soon as can be arranged.' Then he bent and lightly kissed the anxious shape of her mouth. 'And you *will* use *my* name, *querida*,' he vowed as he raised his head again. 'Cristina Scott-Lee has such a staunch Englishness about it, don't you think?'

The barbs were really flying. Head lowering again, so that he could not see her face, Cristina said nothing. What was the use when it was clear he was going to lash out at her whatever she did try to say?

Anton waited, still holding her hand, wishing he had not said that in the cold, nasty way that he had. It was not going to help his cause if he made her hate him enough to walk away—again.

But that wasn't the point, and he knew it wasn't what was really eating away at him. When he'd walked in here and seen her posing in front of the mirror, just as the younger Cristina would have done, his heart had clattered straight through his body to land with a thump at his feet.

Why? Because it had suddenly hit him that he was still in love with her—with that beautiful, vivacious creature flirting with the mirror anyway. He wanted her back, but he couldn't have it like that, and wishing for the impossible was not going to change a single thing. Cristina was still the woman who'd scorned him for an older man six years ago, and he was still the man who wanted revenge.

He dropped her hand.

She lifted her head to look at him. 'Luis—'

No.

He turned away from whatever that look in her eyes was trying to convey to him. 'If you're ready, let's go.'

Cristina stood staring after him. One small peek out of her hiding place and he'd jumped on her, crushed her in his cold iron fist, then stuck a ring on her finger that staked ownership.

In the foyer he stabbed the lift call button. There was a full-length mirror attached to one of the foyer walls and Cristina found her attention caught by it. What she saw was the profile of a tall, dark, excruciatingly handsome and so-phisticated man with the inherent cool and classy bearing of an Englishman mixed with the exotic gold tones of a warm-blooded and tempestuous Brazilian.

'I wish you had never come back.' It was out before she could stop it.

He glanced down, saw her eyes were fixed on the wall and turned his head. It was like clashing head-on with an electrified fence. The green eyes darkened slowly, pouring a heat into her body that dried up the inner surface of her mouth.

What Luis was seeing was beyond Cristina's comprehension, but he came to stand right behind her, hands coming up to clasp her slender upper arms right at the rim of the red sleeves, where they met with the narrow curve of her shoulders. Then he shifted their position until they were facing the mirror full on.

They fitted. They always had fitted together, she thought painfully as she looked at the way the top of her head reached the bow tie at his throat. In every way she was fine-boned delicacy to his muscular dominance. The slenderness of her legs, the fragile curve of her figure in the clinging red dress, even the silken cups of her shoulders, hovering there just above his hands, said *vulnerable woman in the possession of a tall, dark, dominant male*.

He moved—it was hardly anything, but she suddenly felt the jut of erection against her and fell foul of a soft stifled gasp. Her lips parted, red, lush, inviting. Her eyes turned decidedly black. He sent his fingers gliding down the smooth red sleeves to her wrists, then gently pleated them with her own fingers. Cristina watched, held breathless by shimmering sexual tension as he moved their hands to the narrow slopes of her hips then began a slow, slow exploration of her whole body coming to a stop only when both sets of hands were covering her breasts. Eyes fixed in fascination, she felt her nipples tighten against her own palms. It was such a thrilling experience being made to feel the sensual stirring of her own body, that she stood totally breathless, unable to push out a single protest. He moved in that bit closer, and his desire for her was without restraint. Awareness spread like a fine veil across every sense she possessed.

Anton wondered if he was going mad, doing this to them

when they were about to go downstairs and into the public domain, but—

'Look at you,' he rasped out softly. 'You are the most exquisite creature I have ever held this close to me.'

'And you hate yourself for wanting to hold me.'

The two black satin edges of his eyebrows came together across the bridge of his nose. 'Not hate,' he denied, holding her dark eyes with his own disturbingly perplexed ocean green. 'Worried,' he provided. 'If I don't watch out I think you could seriously get me again, and I don't think that would be good for my—'

'Plans?'

He sent her a smile through the mirror—it was like being lit up from inside. 'I was going to say something really soppy—like heart,' he confided, watching her breasts move as her breath caught. Then he added softly, 'But I think that would be just a bit too honest, so we will stick to your word—for now.'

The lift arrived then. Maybe it was fortunate. Any more of this and she would be dragging him back into the suite.

The lift carried them downwards. Cristina stood in front of him, with their clasped hands now pressed to the tiny pulse beating in the flat of her stomach. His mouth arrived to brush a featherlight caress across her throat where it met her shoulder. With a sinuous stretch of fragile muscle she gave him greater access and lost herself in a cloud of sumptuous desire. There wasn't a part of her that had not quickened, not a single inch that did not want to feel the warm brush of his mouth. She moved against him, felt his inner pulse like a living entity.

'Luis.' She breathed his name in the wispy voice of an aroused woman.

That was how their waiting party saw them when the lift doors opened to reveal a tantalisingly beautiful creature dressed in red, lost to the sensual desires of her tall, dark, handsome lover.

CHAPTER EIGHT

CRISTINA, took in the gathered assembly staring at them and felt an icy barb of shock hit her chest. Kinsella was there, dressed in a tube of pale blue fabric that showed off every perfectly neat curve of her long slender shape. Her creamy face was cold, her blue eyes split by a fury she could not contain.

'How could you?' Cristina gasped out accusingly, and tried to stiffen away from him.

He kept her right where she was. 'Listen,' he murmured in what must have looked like a lover's whisper. 'That lady you see standing next to Kinsella is my mother. She is the most important person in the world to me so you will behave like the totally besotted bride-to-be. Understand me?'

Understand? Pulling her gaze away from the angry Kinsella, Cristina looked at the woman who had once been betrothed to Vaasco, and understood so much more than Luis could ever appreciate that the consequences of that understanding were already threatening to squeeze the life out of her sinking, sickly dipping heart.

Maria Ferreira was a beautiful woman of indefinable years, dressed in a beautiful smoky blue silk evening suit that made her look as delicately structured as a fragile rose yet contrarily regal, though she was unable to hide her shocked dismay.

Cristina had not expected this. In the last mad forty-eight hours her mind and her body had been so engrossed in Luis that she just had not once considered the possibility of com-

119

ing face to face with the one person Vaasco had hated above anyone.

And Vaasco had hated.

Swallowing tensely, she tried to turn within Luis's embrace, needing to stop this before it exploded in their faces. But he was not in the mood to listen.

'Behave,' he repeated, kissed her pale cheek, then straightened, releasing only one of her hands as he moved to her side so they could exit the lift.

And it was not by accident that he retained her left hand, bringing two pairs of eyes dipping down to stare at the diamond clustered ruby adorning her finger. It was making a huge statement, Cristina realized, with a growing awareness of the disaster about to descend on their heads.

Recovering her poise first, his mother took a couple of steps forward.

Did she know? Cristina wondered anxiously.

'*Querida*,' Anton greeted her warmly, lowering his dark head to brush his mother's smooth cheek with his lips.

'*Querido—*' his mother responded, returning his embrace.

'You look tired,' he observed as he straightened again. 'Perhaps we should have left this until tomorrow, to give you time to sleep off your jet-lag.'

'I am fine; do not fuss,' his mother said with quiet impatience. 'Although I did assume you and I would be sharing a private dinner, Anton,' she scolded. 'I needed urgently to talk to you, but—'

'You will contain your impatience for another time?' her son suggested with a gentle amusement that made his *mamma*'s eyes flutter—because, like Cristina, she had heard the censure threading through his tone.

'*Meu querida…*' His hand tightened its grip on Cristina's hand to draw her closer. 'Let me introduce you to my mother, Maria Ferreira Scott-Lee—Mother…this beautiful creature is Cristina Vitória de Santa Rosa…Marques…'

The pause, staged for effect, certainly had its reward, Anton noted as he watched his mother's spine rack up in shock.

'You are the daughter of Lorenco Marques?' Maria asked Cristina sharply.

'Y-you knew my father?' Cristina returned, her voice small and very wary.

'We met once—many years ago,' Maria replied in a slightly dazed way. Then her lovely liquid brown eyes narrowed. 'But I was led to believe—'

'You knew Cristina's father?' Anton smoothly took back control. 'Well, this unexpected surprise makes what I have to say next all the more special.' He smiled. 'Mother, you can be the first to congratulate us because the astonishingly beautiful daughter of Lorenco Marques is about to become my wife…'

It was like living in a kind of nightmare after that, one in which people talked and behaved in one way when their body language said entirely something else.

'Well, this is a—surprise.' Luis's mother used dignity to hide behind as she tried not to go pale. 'Congratulations, my dear.' And she even managed to kiss Cristina on both cheeks, when surely she would rather be demanding answers to all the questions that must be whirling around in her head.

Was it Kinsella who had mentioned the Ordoniz name to Luis's mother? Cristina only had to meet the venom in the blue eyes as she politely offered them her congratulations to know that she had.

Only Luis appeared not to notice the undercurrents weaving around them. He smiled, he charmed, he pretended to be the happiest betrothed on this earth. They toasted their coming nuptials with champagne drunk from tall fluted glasses. They moved from the lounge into the restaurant. They discussed food and ordered their individual courses. Luis chose the wine.

And through it all either his hand or his eyes or his mouth were in contact with Cristina somewhere. He toyed with her fingers. If she snatched them beneath the table his followed, captured and tangled with hers, then lifted them up to receive the brush of his mouth before he placed them back on top of the table again. It was like being paraded naked for everyone to stare at, because he was making absolutely no secret of what they would be doing right now if they were not sitting here.

The first course arrived with a flourish from four waiters eager to impress. Cristina looked down at her salad starter and wondered how she was ever going to manage to place a single forkful into her mouth. Her stomach had knotted, the tension in her stretched across every muscle she had. Letting her gaze slip around the table, she saw across the flickering candlelight how difficult his mother was finding it to keep the conversation pleasant and polite.

Kinsella ate sparingly and kept her eyes carefully lowered, but it was what was going on behind the lowered eyelashes that worried Cristina. How could Luis do it to her? How could he make his lover sit here and endure this when only recently she had still been sharing his bed?

He was ruthless. He gave way on nothing, she decided. Did his *mamma* know she had raised this kind of man?

'May I look at your ring, Miss Marques?' Maria Scott-Lee requested.

'Cristina,' her son corrected softly.

Biting her lip in annoyance with him, because his mother was at least *trying* to be nice, Cristina stretched out her hand to display the ring.

Mrs Scott-Lee gazed down at it for a long time before she glanced up at Cristina. 'I have one just like it,' she said with a tense little smile. 'Instead of your beautiful ruby mine has an emerald in the centre—to match the colour of my son's eyes…'

Those eyes belonging to her son narrowed for some reason. His mother refused to look at him. Tension whipped around them all like barbed wire stretched to its optimum. The waiters arrived to remove plates.

While they waited for their main course to arrive, it was Luis's mother who surprised Cristina once again, by mentioning Santa Rosa.

'I visited your home once—a long time ago,' she said. 'It is such a beautiful place.'

Cristina blushed. *'Obrigado,'* she murmured, thinking bleakly, *You would not find much beauty there now*.

'Have you seen Santa Rosa, Anton?' Luis's mother asked her son. 'The ranch sits on the edge of the pampas, with fertile pastures and valleys dramatically backed by the rise of the mountains and the most awe-inspiring sub-tropical forest acting like a barrier to hold back the ocean beyond…'

She went silent for a moment, eyes lost to some distant memory. Then she blinked. 'I may be mistaken, because it was more than thirty years ago when I was there, but I seem to recall that the house itself resembles a Portuguese mansion house?'

Cristina nodded, wetted her dry lips with a sip of wine. 'My ancestors built the house over three hundred years ago. It was not unusual for Portuguese settlers to reproduce the style of house they were used to living in Portugal. The area has many similar-styled houses.'

'But few were built and furnished to the grand style of Santa Rosa, I suspect.'

Cristina lowered her eyes, thinking about the home she

had left only a few short days ago, where grandeur had lost out to peeling paint and damp walls.

'Do you think I might know your mother?'

Cristina shook her head. 'My father met and married my mother when he was visiting Portugal. She died a year later, giving birth to me, so I doubt you would have met.'

'It is a shame, then, that your father could not join us this evening.'

Her tone had taken on a subtle alteration. Everyone noticed it. Luis tensed. Kinsella reached for her wine glass. Cristina waited a moment before she lifted her eyes.

'Both my parents are dead, Senhora Scott-Lee,' she provided, as calmly as she could.

'Ah, my sympathies.' Mrs Scott-Lee tilted her head. 'But surely your father must have married again? Provided you with a brother, perhaps, to inherit Santa Rosa?'

'I am an only child. I inherited Santa Rosa.'

'Then my son has indeed made a fortunate choice in bride,' his mother said. 'Your children will be truly blessed on both sides of the family—unless you have children from your first marriage, who will naturally inherit from you?'

It was like taking a double punch in the stomach. Cristina didn't answer, could not answer. More tension leapt around the table. Kinsella sent her a cold, sly, malicious little smile that chilled Cristina's blood.

'Is there a point to this line of questioning?' Anton intervened at last.

Maria looked at her son. 'I was led to believe that your— betrothed had previously been married.'

'Interesting,' Anton murmured. 'Who exactly led you to believe this?'

She didn't bat an eyelash. 'Miss Lane and I were discussing the interesting fact that you had a—guest staying with you, just before you arrived, *querido*.'

'Miss Lane—' Anton did not so much as cast a glance in Kinsella's direction '—should know better than to discuss my private business with anyone.'

'Even with your mother?'

'I apologise if you feel I've overstepped my working brief, Anton.' Kinsella came in on a contrite little rush. 'But I assumed your mother must already know about—'

'And why should information relayed to you by my secretary make you jump on the first plane out of London to Rio?' Anton continued, right over Kinsella's breathless little rush.

His mother stiffened as she stared at her son. 'Max?' she whispered.

Anton nodded grimly: 'I would also like to know why the fact that Cristina has been married before is of any interest to anyone but Cristina and I, and why you feel it is necessary to interrogate her like this.'

Maria flushed. 'I was merely trying to ascertain—'

'What I was up to?'

'You hardly know the woman, *querido*!' his mother suddenly sparked. 'You met her for the first time barely twenty-four hours ago. She is not what she seems. She is—'

'The widow of Vaasco Ordoniz,' Cristina herself placed into the erupting tension.

'Cristina—'

Ignoring the husky warning in Luis's tone, she looked directly at his mother instead. 'Since you say you knew my father, I must assume that you also knew my husband, Vaasco?'

'He was—'

'I know what he was, Senhora Scott-Lee. I married him; you did not,' Cristina said, and watched as the older woman caught her meaning, then went pale. 'It is therefore perfectly understandable to me, if not to Luis, that you should wish to know why I was willing to marry a man who was more than twice my own age.'

'You misunderstand me—'

'Not at all,' Cristina said. 'I understand you perfectly.'

Luis mother was staring at her with a kind of pained plea glowing in her eyes. She was terrified of what Cristina was going to say next. Kinsella was utterly captivated, and Luis was too calm for her to suspect that he had any idea what was threatening to come out into the open.

But Cristina was not going to be the one to tell him. Let his *mamma* confess her own sins, she thought as she rose to her feet. 'I think I will—'

Her hand was closed inside a male fist. 'Sit down,' Luis instructed.

'Anton—' his *mamma* said on a hushed warning breath. The altercation at their table was beginning to attract attention, other diners were turning to stare.

A man appeared at Cristina's side. Young, slight and immaculately dressed. 'Excuse me for interrupting your dinner, *senhora*,' he murmured politely. 'I have been instructed to give this to you…'

He handed Cristina a white envelope. Amidst the rest of what was happening around her it made the whole scene take on a surreal quality as the young man bowed politely, then melted away again.

'What the hell was that about?' Anton demanded.

His guess was as good as anyone's—except for Cristina's. She took one glance at the envelope, went as white as a sheet, then turned on a muffled, 'Excuse me,' stepped around her chair and fled.

Anton shot to his feet to go after her. His mother was on her feet too. 'No, Anton,' she said quickly. 'I think Miss Marques needs to read her letter alone.'

Not while I'm here to stop her, Anton thought grimly, and went to go after her.

'You cannot enter the Ladies' Room, darling!' his mother said anxiously.

'I will go if you like.'

It was enough to make Anton's head whip around. 'You will remain right where I can see you, Miss Lane!' he lanced at his so called private secretary.

Kinsella blanched at his tone. His mother gasped. They were all on their feet now and people were openly staring.

Frustration bit into him. This had all gone wrong. How had he let it go so wrong?

His mind shot back to the call from Max. Until then he had been firmly focused on what he was doing and why he was doing it. Everything had been running smoothly and under his control. Then Max's call had arrived to muddy the waters, and the arrival of his mother had muddied them some more. The machinations of Kinsella, the burning leap of angry jealousy that had come with Max's wisecrack about the Ordoniz widow—and seeing the stranger in the shopping mall when he thought he'd sharpened his focus. In truth, that was the moment he'd lost what bit of focus he'd had left.

This dinner was supposed to have been a trial by demonstration, aimed to show his mother and Kinsella Lane that, no matter what they thought or wanted or hoped to the contrary, he and Cristina were an inseparable item. Whatever else needed to be said should have taken place in private. Why would he want to turn it into a public scene? Why would he want to embarrass Cristina in front of anyone? She was the woman he was going to marry, the woman he—

Dear God. It hit him then, the one thing he had been carefully skirting around without actually grasping with both hands. It had been there staring at him from the moment he saw her across the crowded reception room. Further back, when he'd stood staring at her name typed in bold on a document and felt himself coming alive. He'd even fooled himself into thinking he was still in love with a memory when he'd watched her pose in her red dress, but it was no distant memory. It was here and now and so potent he could actually taste it!

He must have looked strange because his mother placed a hand on his arm to capture his attention, and when he looked at her he saw concern there, a mother's instinctive understanding wrapped in dark-eyed remorse.

'I will go and see if Cristina is all right,' she said gently.

The letter. His mind spun. What was in the letter? Who was it from? Why would one look at the envelope make Cristina turn and run? His chest grew tight, as if a steel band was trying to squeeze down a searing hot desire to explode into panic. But there were other issues here that had to be dealt with—Kinsella Lane being the most pressing one.

He caught his mother's hand as she went to follow Cristina. 'She is the most important thing in the world to me, so you treat her with respect—understand?'

His mother pressed her lips together and nodded while the words he'd just uttered played a taunting echo inside his head.

Anton took in air, and by the time he had released it again and turned his attention to Kinsella he had himself back in control.

'Right, let's make this more formal, Miss Lane,' he enunciated with ice-tipped authority. 'We will take our business upstairs to the conference room, I think.'

Then he turned to stride across the restaurant, ignoring all the curious looks he was receiving and pausing by the *maître d'* to sign a hastily produced bill for their ruined dinner. As he moved on towards the lifts he took out his cellphone to call his two executives to the conference room. He wanted witnesses to what was coming next.

'Anton, please listen to me.' Kinsella's hand arrived on the sleeve of his jacket, the soft, slightly pleading tone in her voice making his skin start to creep. 'You don't understand. Your mother made it impossible for me to—'

'You would be wise to keep your mouth shut until we gain privacy,' he bit right across her, thinking Cristina was right; she did flutter around him like a fluffy moth. He swatted her hand away, then walked into the lift.

Cristina was sitting in a chair, staring at the unopened envelope she clutched in her fingers. It was addressed to Cristina Ordoniz, which was enough to turn her stomach, but what was really choking her of any ability to open the letter was the logo neatly printed on the corner of the envelope.

Javier Estes and Associates, it said. *Advocates of Law.*

Vaasco's lawyers. How many of these awful white envelopes had she received in the months after Vaasco's death? Each one of them had carried only bad news. Each one had turned her into this trembling, shaking person she was now.

But the letters had stopped a long time ago—long before her father had died. Why start again now? And why receive it hand-delivered right in the middle of a busy restaurant?

The only way to find out was to open it, she told herself, then swallowed and made her fingers break the seal and draw out the single sheet of paper that was inside.

Shock hit then—the kind of totally bewildering stunning shock that twisted her brain into complete knots. The letter was not to do with her late husband's estate at all. Senhor

Estes had more than one client—of course he did, she told herself. But—Enrique Ramirez?

Her stomach rolled and kept on rolling as she read in growing disbelief what it was she had been handed.

A bequest, it said, and named a figure that scrambled her brain all the more. Enrique Ramirez had bequeathed her just enough money to save Santa Rosa.

Just enough to pay off her debts.

Dared she believe it? The letter had been delivered in a very unconventional manner. Maybe it was a joke—a very sick joke. Maybe she would be wise checking out the source before she—

The door suddenly opened and she looked up just to stare as Luis's mother walked in.

'Are you all right?' Mrs Scott-Lee questioned warily.

'No.' It was no use pretending she was when she wasn't.

'You feel ill? The letter—distressed you?'

The letter, Cristina thought, is a dream come true.

Except for one unattainable dream. 'I think I need to go to my room,' she whispered.

'Of course,' Luis's mother said, walking towards her. 'I will take you there—' Then she stopped, hesitation in every line of her slender, elegant frame. 'You know about Vaasco and me, don't you?' she thrust out suddenly.

Cristina nodded. 'You were betrothed to him, but you had an affair with another man. This man.'

Cristina held out the letter. Pale as herself now, hands as unsteady as her own hands, Luis's mother took the letter, lowered her eyes and began to read.

'Ramirez again,' she breathed after a long silence, then on a heavy sigh she folded into the chair next to Cristina's.

Cristina did not know what to say to her. When you possessed the knowledge that a woman of Luis's mother's stature had had some wild affair beneath the very roof of her then betrothed, words just refused to come.

'You knew Enrique well for him to leave you this money?'

The money. Cristina sucked in a deep breath as her stomach rolled again. She knew why it kept doing that. She understood exactly why she was feeling sickly instead of jumping for joy.

'I met him only once,' she replied. 'He—he saved my life when I was very little... Why did Luis mention his name to me?'

'Anton,' his *mamma* corrected absently.

For some crazy reason, in this mixed-up situation, Cristina heard herself laugh. 'I know his name, *senhora*,' she said dryly. 'I have known his name for a long time— for six years, in fact, since we first met and fell in love and then—' *Lost each other,* she tagged on silently

'You mean—*you* are the one?' Maria Scott-Lee was staring at her oddly.

'The one?' Cristina frowned.

So did Luis's mother. 'Nothing.' She looked away. 'Forget I mentioned it.'

Silence tumbled. And, in the way that everything had been happening in its own peculiar way tonight, the silence was not tense or tight or hostile, as it should have been. It was just—silent.

'You love my son?' Mrs Scott-Lee asked suddenly.

I refuse to answer that, Cristina thought. 'I will not be marrying him, if that is where this is leading.'

'But why not? What is wrong with Anton that you turn him down not once but twice?'

'Who said that I turned him down twice?' Cristina asked sharply.

'No one. My mistake.' His mother was frowning again. 'Why are you saying you will not marry him?'

For a million unutterable reasons, she thought hollowly—but named only one. 'Well, he's a womaniser, if you must know.'

'Of course he enjoys the company of women,' his *mamma* defended loyally. 'He is young and handsome and possesses a perfectly healthy sexual appetite. However, when Anton marries he will have the good manners to stay faithful to his wife!'

The good manners? Cristina released another of those laughs. It would take more than good manners to make Luis keep the zip on his pants shut!

'He spent the night before last in the arms of another woman.'

'I do not believe you.'

'His secretary informs me that she and Luis have been lovers for months.'

'Miss Lane?' For some reason Luis's mother sounded thoroughly shaken. 'I sincerely hope that you are wrong about that,' she murmured unsteadily.

'Well, I'm not.'

The threat of tears came then. Cristina got up, the fool inside her giving way to a heartbreaking bout of common sense.

'Give this to Luis and show him the letter,' she said huskily, removing the ring and dropping it gently on his *mamma*'s lap. 'He will understand.'

Then she turned to leave.

'He will not let you go,' Mrs Scott-Lee fed after her.

'That is no longer his choice to make!' Cristina choked.

'Anton does not have a choice!' Maria stood up—letter and ring clasped in one hand, the other closing on Cristina's arm. 'He has to marry you, Cristina, or he will not inherit from his father.'

His father? Cristina twisted round. 'What are you talking about? His father has been dead for six years!'

'I don't mean—' Mrs Scott-Lee stopped herself, then uttered a soft, unladylike curse. 'He will not forgive me for this,' she whispered. 'He is not going to forgive me for my interference anyway, but...' She looked at Cristina. 'Please sit down again,' she invited unevenly. 'I need to explain some things to you...'

Anton's face-off with Kinsella was not a pleasant one. Having been cornered by her own machinations, his loyal secretary gave it to him hook, line and spitting venom. Then, with his two young executives standing by as witnesses, he went on to formally dismiss her from his employment on the grounds of gross misconduct.

'Do you think you can do this to me when I've devoted the last six years of my life to you?' she attacked. 'From the day that you stepped into your dead father's shoes I have been working hard to turn myself into everything you could possibly want!'

'But I don't want what you are,' Anton denounced brutally.

'No.' Kinsella quivered in disgust. 'You prefer a black-haired witch who was more than willing to fall into bed with you the first chance she was handed!'

How Anton kept his hands from closing around her throat he had no idea. 'You see, Miss Lane,' he responded icily, 'the difference between you wanting to fall into my bed and my wanting *any* other woman there is that *they* are desirable and *you* are not.'

'And *she* is so good at playing the whore, isn't she?' Kinsella spat back. 'But then she is a woman who is willing to do anything to get what she wants, even marry a fat and withered old man! I wonder if she crawled all over him like I watched her crawling all over you!'

White now, knocked back on his heels by that last venomous spit, Anton glanced at the connecting door, securely shut at the moment whereas yesterday it had been left swinging wide open. An icy sensation crept down his spine as his mind replayed a sequence of events that should have been private to him and Cristina.

But Kinsella had walked into this conference room and coolly followed the trail of discarded clothing to the bedroom. His skin began to crawl as he imagined her standing in the bedroom doorway watching them and listening, like some sick bloody voyeur, before quietly walking out again to go and snoop in his private files before calling up his mother.

He felt sick. *She* was sick. He turned his back on her. 'Get her out of here,' he rasped at the two other men.

Striding into his suite five minutes later, he found his mother sitting tensely on the edge of a chair. She jumped up. 'Anton—'

'Where is Cristina?' he demanded.

'I—we need to talk first,' his mother said, her eyes pleading with him in a way that locked up every single bone he possessed.

'Where is she?' he bit out, and spun towards the bedrooms. He wanted to know what was in that damn letter. He wanted to know what it was that had made her run like that!

'She's gone!' His mother's shaking voice froze him. 'Sh-she has gone home to Santa Rosa, *querido*. She—'

All his life he had loved this woman, without exception, but when he turned on her now Anton understood why his mother took a jerky step back.

'If you've talked her into leaving me I will never forgive you,' he grated.

'She left of her own volition, I promise you,' Maria vowed painfully. 'I might be a foolish woman, Anton, but I—' She stopped to swallow thickly. 'She said for me to tell you that she will be in touch with you to explain when she feels that she can.'

'Feels that she can *what*?' he bit back as an old bitterness began to well up inside him.

Then it sank in. Cristina had gone. The tension holding him released its grip and he turned from his mother as a violent shudder racked his frame.

Gone—again. Left him—*again*.

'She claims that Miss Lane is your lover,' Maria explained unsteadily. 'Anton, has learning about your real father meant a thing to you? Enrique flipped from woman to woman! He enjoyed them—yes! But he died an unhappy and lonely man!'

'I don't want to hear about him,' he gritted.

'Yet it is because of him that you are here!'

'What a joke.' He laughed, swinging back round again. 'You know, *querida*, I never so much as clapped eyes on Enrique Ramirez but I think he knew me better than you do or even than I know myself!' He took in a deep breath. It hurt to do it. 'I am here for Cristina. I'm in love with Cristina. I have always—damn *always* been in love with Cristina!'

A hand shot up to cover his mouth.

It was an act so unfamiliar to both of them, 'Oh, *Meu Dues*,' his mother choked, and sank down into the chair.

Anton dragged the hand away again. 'I'm going after her—'

'No, Anton, please wait!' She shot up again. 'There are some things I need to explain to you before you do that...'

CHAPTER NINE

CRISTINA was busy by the main barn when a sound made her look up to watch a helicopter fly overhead. It circled the homestead a couple of times before deciding to drop down into an empty paddock out of her field of sight.

It had to be Luis. She did not do much as even consider the possibility that it could be anyone else. He would be arriving for their last big confrontation, though she had not expected him to get here quite so soon.

A frisson slid through her. She had to give her determination a hard tug not to react to the sting of electric excitement and, tightening the softness of her mouth, she returned to what she had been doing. But she felt his approach like long icy fingers curling themselves around her until she could not take in a single breath.

Anton came to a halt several feet away, watching in silence as she hefted bales of hay from the barn to the truck while Pablo, her helper, eyed them both warily from beneath the brim of his hat. She was wearing work-faded jeans and a check shirt. Heavy work gloves protected her hands. Her hair was lost beneath a red spotted headscarf and her face was bare of everything but its smooth golden skin. She looked too delicate to touch, yet she hefted those bales of hay like a man.

Clenching his body across the rush of anger that hit it, he stepped closer, flicked the helper a look that sent him scuttling away, then turned his attention to Cristina.

'Look at me,' he commanded.

Her response was to bend, with the intention of hefting

up yet another bale, and in biting frustration Anton stepped forward and placed his foot down on it. He watched her go still, watched her eyelashes flicker when she took in his black leather hand-stitched shoes and the cut of his black silk trousers. The tension between them heightened the higher those eyes drifted, taking in the black silk dinner jacket hanging open to reveal the fine white dress-shirt he still wore beneath.

If looks could paint a picture then the expression on her face was a masterpiece of a woman totally riveted by what she was seeing.

'Impressed?' he said, bringing her eyes up that bit further, to the open collar of his shirt, where the rich golden skin at his throat was glossed with the sheen of sweat. His bowtie still hung there, like a trailing piece of black ribbon.

'It took hours of negotiation to get the helicopter charter company to let me fly myself,' he supplied, with hard, harsh, husky bite. 'Before that I had to get to Sao Paulo—and I was right on your stubborn tail until then, *meu querida*,' he informed her. 'Count yourself lucky that I was delayed, or you might have found yourself prostrate by now on this bale with my fingers wrapped around your slender throat. Instead I find I don't have the energy. I'm hot, I'm tired, and I'm in dire need of a shower and a shave—'

Her eyes flicked to the stubble covering the cleft in his chin. Her lips parted, that vulnerable upper lip just begging—begging for it.

His own lips flexed.

'I need a drink so badly my throat thinks it's been cut, and some food inside me would be pleasant, since you effectively ruined dinner last night...'

Then, just to make sure that his next point went home,

he bent low enough to bring his eyes into full contact with her darker than black eyes, vulnerable, wishful—sad.

His teeth came together. 'In other words, sweetheart, what you see here is a man at the end of his rope. So be warned that ignoring me right now is a very—very dangerous thing to do.'

She blinked, she swallowed, and her lips quivered as she took in a small breath. He nodded, held her eyes for a moment longer, and thought about kissing her utterly, totally—*punishingly* breathless, but then straightened up and took his foot off the bale.

It was then that she saw his overnight bag, dumped on the ground. He watched her look at it, then pull in a breath. 'Luis—'

'Anton,' he corrected, turning his back on her to take an interest in his surroundings. 'I don't feel much like Luis right now.'

He could almost hear her lips snapping shut before they opened again.

'I will not marry you.'

'Fine.' He shrugged. 'Now, show me round this heavy investment I've bought into.'

'Will you listen to me?'

He swung back, everything about him hard like iron. 'Only when you have something to say that I want to hear.'

'I don't need your money any more! Did your mother not tell you?'

'About my father's bequest to you?'

'Father—?' She stared at him.

Anton returned the look with an inscrutability that said he was not going to play that game. 'You know that Enrique Ramirez was my father because my mother told you. Now that we have that attempt at yet more deception out of the way, will you show me around—please?'

Please. Cristina looked at this tall, dark, arrogant man, with his beautiful accent and his beautiful manners and the hard crystal eyes that warned her to beware. She felt that oh, so helpless, *I do so love you, Luis* lump form in her throat, and—

'I can pay my debts.' She stuck to her guns, chin up, eyes defiant.

'You can try,' he invited with a thin smile. 'But the moment you so much as attempt to pay me off, I will sell all your debts on to the Alagoas Consortium so fast your head will spin. They will not be so easy to please as I am.'

He would do it too. Cristina could see the cold intent cast like armour on his face.

'You are not easy to please.' She sighed wearily, then turned away from him to remove her gloves so she could toss them down onto the bale of hay.

Without looking at him again she walked over to the hand pump beside the barn and set cool water flowing to wash her hands, then pulled the scarf off her head and wet it to use to cool her sweat-sheened face and throat.

If Luis thought he'd had a bad day then he should have lived hers, she thought tiredly. Three ranch hands had walked off the job the moment she'd left for Rio, leaving Pablo alone to do the jobs of four—five, if she counted herself. They had not been paid in months, so how could she complain about them walking away? And when she'd entered the house she'd found Orraca, the housekeeper, on her hands and knees mopping up the kitchen which had flooded due to a burst pipe. Orraca was too old to be on her hands and knees, so Cristina had taken over the mopping while Pablo fixed the leaky pipe. Then she and Pablo had come out here, to start catching up on the jobs that had not been done. Now it was two o'clock in the afternoon, the sun was at its hottest, and all she wanted to do was to take that shower Luis had mentioned, crawl into her bed and sleep…for a hundred years if she could.

A hand came out to take the wet scarf from her. It was stupid for her lips to start quivering, but they did. Luis drenched the scarf again, folded it carefully, then placed it carefully around her neck.

A sob rolled in her throat. 'Don't be nice to me,' she protested, having to blink the tears back.

'You'd prefer my hands there instead of the scarf?' he quizzed. 'Or maybe you would like it better if I just turned round and left again.'

Cristina's mouth opened but nothing came out. His hands dropped to her shoulders, and it just was not fair that he pulled her close. Before she knew what she was doing two sets of fingers had crept up in between them and were toying with the black ribbon edges of his bowtie, which were dangling either side of the tantalising V of damp skin exposed at his glistening throat.

'I'm in your blood,' he murmured huskily. 'You are in mine. Why keep fighting it?'

Because I have to, she thought, and moved away from him, lifting her chin and taking in a deep breath.

'Do you want some refreshment?' she asked then.

'Or something?' he drawled by return.

Her eyes gave a warning flash. 'Do you?' she persisted.

His turn to utter a sigh as he glanced at his watch, then gave a shake of his head. 'If you're going to show me around the place then we don't have time for food and drink. There's a weather front coming in,' he explained. 'I would rather use the helicopter to see Santa Rosa from the air while we can…'

It was a complete refusal to give in to anything, Cristina noted. Standing here, looking at him, stubbornly willing to continue the fight, she caught the signs of tiredness around his eyes, and for the first time the hint of strain playing with the corners of his mouth.

And she surrendered—for now.

Time later to be stubborn again, she told herself, as without another word she turned to seek out Pablo, who was still standing in the shadow of the barn, and ask him to take Luis's bag into the house.

With a very hooded look at Luis, and a nod of his head to her, Pablo complied. Cristina knew that by the time they arrived back here the whole of Santa Rosa would know that she had been steamrollered by a man.

Luis took off his jacket and with a polite 'Thank you' handed it to Pablo to take inside with his bag. By then Cristina had unearthed a bottle of water from the chiller she kept in the truck. Silently she handed the bottle to Luis, and he drank thirstily on the way to the helicopter. Ten minutes later they were in the air, and Cristina was quietly explaining what they could see while he sat beside her, listening, asking shrewd questions and controlling the helicopter as if he had been born to do it.

Which he probably had, she thought ruefully.

Anton listened to the way her voice began to soften as she described what lay beneath them. And he understood why her voice did that. Santa Rosa was a stunning place of breathtaking contrasts.

They flew over wide open plains scattered with cattle and the occasional gaucho, then on to the first change in scenery as they swept over rich green meadows threaded with gushing streams not quite wide enough to be called rivers but impressive nonetheless. She directed him to fly over a hill and into a valley dotted with small neat whitewashed houses, each surrounded by their own small plot of land.

'This is part of Santa Rosa?'

Cristina nodded. 'The valley beneath us is the land the Alagoas Consortium wants to turn into a spur from the highway to the forest,' she explained, and Anton did not need telling what the people who lived in the whitewashed houses down there would be losing if the developers had their way.

Then she directed him to fly over the other side of the valley. Almost instantly Anton saw exactly why she had instructed him to come this way. Even before they rose above the valley rim he saw the forest rising up like a huge dark wall in front of them. Majestic, invincible...or so you would like to think. But from up here it didn't take words for him to see what was so valuable to the developers. A natural fault in the earth's crust had carved a deep groove in the forest that stretched for miles and miles towards what he saw in the misted distance was the sea.

'This is it?' he said, as they tracked along the fine vein of water that threaded the base of the groove.

'*Sim.*'

'What happens to the river when the rains come?'

'It floods.'

'So what do they intend to do with the flood when they build their road?'

Not if but when, Cristina noted with a shiver. 'They plan to run their road along either side of it, above the flood line.'

Her eyes scanned the area of forest that would have to be demolished to achieve such an aim. Beside her she could feel Luis doing the same thing.

'The banker in me says what a goldmine you're sitting on. The human in me says what a sick, criminal waste,' was his only comment.

Cristina said nothing. And that was how it remained between them as they made the journey back the way they had come. They landed back in the paddock behind the house, but not before Anton had circled the two-storeyed plaster-walled mansion house. He said nothing about its poor state of repair, but his mouth maintained a flat line as he settled them back down to earth again.

The heat of the afternoon was intense, and the silence between them all the more so—growing as they walked towards the house, passing the collection of ageing barns and paddocks as they did. The house itself was surrounded by a low whitewashed wall which sectioned it off from the rest of Santa Rosa. An open archway took them into gardens that would once have been beautiful but had, like the house itself, fallen into decay.

They hadn't seen a single living soul since they landed. 'It's very quiet,' he remarked.

'Siesta time,' Cristina murmured.

Now, there's an idea, Anton mused, but kept the thought to himself.

The tension between them grew even stronger when they entered the coolness of the house itself. Without another word passing between them Cristina led the way across a high-ceilinged hallway and up a wide, gracefully curving flight of stairs. Anton looked around him at the once elegant but now scuffed and chipped tiled floor, and the walls hung with heavy-framed oils that looked as if they'd seen much better days.

Mentally crossing her fingers that Orraca had instructed Pablo to place Luis's bag in the only useable guest bedroom out of twelve, Cristina pushed open the door.

His bag sat, on the heavily carved ottoman, she saw with relief and stepped aside to allow him to precede her inside.

'There is a bathroom through the connecting door,' she told him, in a cool level tone that just did not reflect what was trying its best to erupt inside her. 'I will organise something to eat and drink for when you come back downstairs.'

He did not say a single word, just stood inside the room looking around him. Cristina closed the door with a quiet, dignified click and then swung herself back against the nearest wall. Eyes tight shut, heart dipping and diving, breasts heaving beneath her damp and sticky shirt, she refused, absolutely, to look at why she was feeling like this.

Then, right on the back of that refusal, she was pushing away from the wall and running like a crazy woman down the stairs, across the hall and into the kitchen, situated at the rear of the house. She still did not allow herself to think about what she was doing as she snatched up a tray and laid it on the kitchen table. Two minutes later she had added a small freshly baked loaf of crusty bread, fruit conserve, a pitcher of chilled lemonade from the refrigerator, and the plate of sliced fresh fruit she'd spied in there. Then, as a last impulse she flew down into the wine cellar and plucked at random one of her father's bottles of wine and added it, a bottle opener and two glasses to the tray.

Sad, weak, pathetic, she castigated herself when she eventually picked up the tray and made her way back to the stairs again. *'Triste, fraco, patético,'* she repeated beneath her breath, just to make sure she got the point.

In the bedroom Anton was experiencing a similar overload—of the masculine kind which translated into tight-chested, gut-gripping anger beneath his own sweat-soaked shirt.

This place was like some cracked and crumbling forgotten museum. How long had she been living here on her own, rattling around it like the resident ghost with no life worth speaking of? Where did she get off, preferring this to marriage and a full life with him?

He yanked his shirt off over his head and used it to wipe the sweat from his face, then tossed it angrily to the ground. It landed in a float of expensive silk on top of a worn Persian carpet that must have once cost the earth.

Well, not any more, he thought grimly as the rest of his clothes joined the shirt. The carpet, like the faded satin coverlet on the bed and the matching curtains at the windows, needed a hasty burial—along with the rest of this time-locked place.

Unzipping his bag, he hunted down his toilet bag and headed for the connecting door. Half expecting to find a cast iron tub with a pitcher of water standing beside it, it did not mollify his feelings one iota to discover a fully functional if old-fashioned set of sanitary units waiting for him. He turned on the shower suspended over the white bathtub and grimaced his surprise when it gushed clear water into the bath. Then, with a sigh, he turned his attention to removing the growth from his face.

He did not know what was coming next—hell, he did not want to think about what was coming next if it meant yet another battle to get her to see some damn sense. But his insides were already revving up for it, stinging and tensing and—girding, he thought with yet another tight grimace.

Cristina was functioning on a different level by the time she'd carried the tray upstairs and arrived outside the bedroom door. Balancing the tray on one arm, she grabbed her lower lip between her teeth, then gave a knock on the door before twisting the handle and pushing it open.

Luis was not there. Her tummy muscles twisted with what might have been relief, though she wasn't sure. As she placed the tray down on a table by the window she could hear the shower running, and that was when she saw his clothes lying in a heap on the floor.

Was she going to do it?

Those muscles twisted again. Her heart did the same nervous trick because—yes, she *was* going to it. *Just* this once—just this once she was going to do what she really wanted to do and act out a dream that had haunted her for six long years, which involved Luis, this house and that bed.

Her clothes landed on the top of his clothes. With trembling fingers she released her hair from its topknot, then on impulse bent to snatch up Luis's bowtie and used it to loop her loosened hair back from her face.

The knock sounded as Anton was drying his face with a threadbare but spotlessly clean towel. He turned to stare as the door opened, then went completely still when a perfectly naked Cristina stepped inside, closed the door again, then turned to look at him.

She just looked. He just looked. Both of them held in tight stasis that knew exactly where to centre itself. Her chin was up and her dark eyes were defensive, her soft, lush, beautiful mouth quivering and as vulnerable as hell.

Now she had come this far Cristina did not know what to do or say next to make something happen. If he rejected her she would die where she stood. Water hissed from behind the plastic curtain drawn across the bath, steam swirled and eddied, to say that the ancient boiler had not let her down as it often did.

He recognised his bowtie holding her hair back and his eyelashes flickered across the darkening green of his eyes.

'I thought we could share the shower,' she heard herself say in a breathless little voice. 'Do you mind?'

Did he mind? Anton mocked. For the first time in six

years she had come to him, and it did not need words on his part to tell her how he felt about that. She only had to dip her eyes to the cluster of black curls surrounding his sex to know whether he minded her coming to him like this.

The pink tip of her tongue appeared as she looked at him. The physical response his body gave brought her eyes flickering back to his face. Without uttering a single word he reached out with one hand and swept back the plastic curtain, watched the tight little pull of air she took before she could peel herself away from the door.

Suddenly stupidly shy, Cristina slewed her eyes away from him and turned to put out a hand to test the heat of the water spraying out of the shower head. It was too hot; she adjusted it. His hands arrived on her hips as she did so, the jut of his sex making its bold statement against her while he waited for her to be very practical and get the water temperature just right. For some reason the situation caught her with a compulsive giggle, and from behind her she heard his low, deep, husky laugh.

The tension broke, just like that, and he was lifting her up against him to latch his teeth to her shoulder while he stepped into the bath. Water poured down her front, the curtain was swept shut, steam fogged her vision and Luis fogged up everything else.

He touched, he stroked, he moulded her to him, following the streams of water. She responded by lifting up her arms to curve them around his neck and turned her face so she could claim his mouth. When that was no longer enough she twisted to face him, and that was when the really serious kissing and stroking began.

He filled her hands and she stroked him gently. His hand slipped between her thighs. They made love to each other with their mouths and their fingers until both were barely on the planet, but he was not going to let this be over as quickly as that, because once it was over neither knew what was waiting beyond, and they didn't want to know.

So he soothed things down by locating the soap, and began washing her all over while she stood gazing up at him with heavy, dark, love-drugged eyes. *'Luis, Luis,'* she kept on saying. He wondered if she was aware at all that she said his name like a whispered call to a lost lover. I'm here, he wanted to say, but was too afraid of breaking into the spell that was holding them both.

Instead he handed her the soap and then stood and just enjoyed while she washed him, caressed him, until he could stand it no longer and he switched off the shower and stepped out of the bath. He wrapped a towel each around them, then lifted her into his arms to carry her into the bedroom.

His eyes blazed when he saw that the covers had been stripped back from the bed. She'd planned this, had known they were going to end up here. This beautiful, stubborn contrary woman, who was her own worst enemy, pushed him away with one hand and hooked him right back to her with the other.

They fell on the bed in a spray of clean water droplets, rough towelling and deep, hungry kisses. They made love while the afternoon sun dropped lower in the sky. And when it was over it wasn't over, because they still touched, kissed, drew out the after-loving like a trailing silken thread, until hunger and thirst sent her leaping off the bed to pick up the tray.

She'd forgotten nothing. Anton smiled as she placed the tray on the flat of the bed between them, then gave him the wine bottle to open while she knelt beside him, golden, slender, totally carefree in her nakedness, as she broke off chunks of bread and smeared them with conserve, offering

him a piece, then smiling at him as he handed her the wine
to pour while he bit into the bread. His bowtie had managed
to stay in her hair, though he didn't know how it had,
considering what they had been doing. She looked loved
and lovely, lips soft and swollen from his kisses, the swing
of her nipples dark and tight.

She offered him a glass of wine. He took it and drank,
then his face instantly contorted at the harsh, brackish taste.

'My God, you're trying to poison me,' he gasped.

To his shock, huge glistening tears filled her eyes.

'What did I say?' he demanded in bewilderment, then
saw the way she was staring at his glass of wine.
'Christina…' He sighed. 'Don't be such a baby. I was jok-
ing! Here—try the wine,' he invited. 'I can guarantee it
will knock your eyes out.'

She shook her head, mouth small now, and trembling,
those tear-filled eyes too big in her face. Anger roared up
like a monster inside him. Who the hell had knocked the
spirit out of her to the extent that she could almost fall
apart over a glass of poor wine?

That bastard Ordoniz?

He tossed the rest of the wine to the back of his throat
and swallowed, then slammed the glass back down on the
tray.

'All right,' he said then. 'Let's talk about this. Since
when did you get this upset over a lousy glass of wine,
instead of just tossing your own glassful into my face for
being so insensitive?'

'I wanted it to be perfect.'

'Wanted *what* to be perfect?'

'This…' She stared at the bed, the tray—him. 'You, me,
here—our last time together,' she whispered.

Our last time…

The rumbling beginnings of their next major battle began

to roll around the room. Anton tried to hold it back by clamping his lips together and clenching just about every muscle he could. But it was not going to happen. Anger six long years in the fermenting, it was filling with a bitterness that by far outstripped the taste of the wine.

'So this—' he flicked a hand at the tray '—the surprise visit to the bathroom and the rest—was just for the sex, was it?'

'No—'

'A last good old frolic with your Englishman before you kicked him out of your life again?'

'Y-you—'

'I've had it,' he announced, and launched himself right off the bed.

'Luis—no!' she cried. The look he sent her had her scrambling off the bed. 'You don't understand!'

'What's to understand? I've noticed the pattern here. Have you noticed it?' he rasped. 'You run; I follow. You take the sex. You run again—or in this case you kick me out.'

'I don't mean it to be like that—'

'No?' He released a hard laugh, dragged on a pair of pale chinos and zipped them up. 'I've offered to marry you—again,' he delivered. 'I've offered to save this bloody awful place. I've *given* you the sex! Who is the fool here, do you think? You or me?'

This time she didn't answer. Reaching out, he picked up a white T-shirt and dragged it on over his head.

'And of course I must not forget that you have other options now,' he continued bitterly. 'Enrique Ramirez has seen to that.'

'Y-you said—'

'What did I say?' he lanced at her, ignoring—refusing—to see the way she was standing there naked, shivering, face as white as the worn sheet on the bed. 'That I would sell you out to the Alagoas Consortium if you tried to pay me back? Do I really come over to you as the kind of bastard who would do that to you?'

Without wanting a reply, he ripped out a sigh and went hunting for a clean pair of socks in his bag. He came out with another folded white T-shirt and tossed it at her.

'Cover yourself,' he said, as if he hated the very sight of her body now—and turned his back on the next pained look that crossed her face and sat down on the bed to pull on his socks. 'You married a man old enough to be your father to save all of this once. I would love to know why you could not bring yourself to do the same thing with me.'

'You are not old.'

'So you've come to *prefer* older men, is that it? Does their lined and sagging flesh turn you on?'

If only you knew, Cristina thought painfully as she pulled on the T-shirt, emerging from its clean white folds to have her breath catch in her throat at the sight of him. Fully dressed now, and standing at the end of the bed grimly stuffing clothes into his bag, his height and the lean muscle power beneath the casual clothes hit her harder than the sight of him in one of his smart business suits had ever done.

'You look very much the Latino,' she remarked helplessly.

'I am English,' he declared. 'To the last drop of my blood.'

'You never used to deny your Brazilian side,' she whispered. 'You—'

'Well, now I do deny it!' Rocking her back with a fresh blast of his anger, he swung away from her, then violently back again, hard lines suddenly raking his lean face. 'Six years ago you rejected me because my *Englishness* did not appeal to you. You didn't want to move to England and play the banker's wife. You did not want to rear English children who would have their natural passions bred out of them.'

Like a machine gun he shot her with all the hateful words she had thrown at him six years ago.

'Finding out that my real father was a Brazilian does not alter the person I am inside, Cristina. I still *am* an Englishman who *thinks* like an Englishman.' Hard fingers made a tight, stabbing gesture at his head. 'And I promise you that I will go back to England and marry an Englishwoman, remain this English banker who will rear English banker children, while you—' he made a gesture of derision '—get your dearest wish.'

With that he bent to zip his bag up, cursed when he remembered his soap bag, still languishing in the bathroom, and strode that way, leaving Cristina standing there white-faced and shaken, stripped to the very bones by her own cruel lies.

A shudder raked her slender body, a hand jerking up to cover her mouth in guilt-ridden dismay at the cruelty she had used six years ago to make Luis walk away.

She had mocked his English upbringing, his public school accent and his stuffy banker family. She had scorned his offer of marriage and demanded to know where he had got the idea that what they had was anything but a temporary affair. Cringeing inside, she had listened to her own voice demolish everything they'd spent a whole year cherishing.

Then she had just walked away.

This time Luis was going to do it. And she could see in the hard set of his face as he strode back to his bag that this time he would not come back.

He zipped the bag up again, ignoring her as he straightened and turned for the door.

Oh, *Meu Dues*, she thought. He was going.

It hit like a thunderbolt. 'No,' she wrenched out, and moved like lightning, racing past him to stand with her back against the door. 'I need you to listen while I tell you something.'

His wide shoulders tensed—his back, his whole body. He did not look into her eyes and she knew—*knew*—he did not want to look at her ever again.

'Move out of the way, Cristina,' he instructed grimly.

'Please,' she begged him. 'You must understand before you go why I cannot marry you!'

Fury leapt in his eyes. He took a step towards her. 'If you say that to me one more time—'

'I lied to you Luis!' she cried out. 'Everything I said to you six years ago was just one big wicked lie! I never, ever wanted to hurt you. I have always loved you more than anything else in this world! But I am not what you need! Your mother said—'

'My mother?' he lanced at her. 'What the hell has she got to do with this?'

'Nothing.' She had not meant to say that. 'Sh-she loves you.'

'Great,' he snapped. 'So everyone loves me.' The bag dropped to the floor as he threw out his arms in an arc of blistering contempt. 'So what am I supposed to say to that life-changing statement, Cristina? Oh, that's okay, then. *Now* I don't mind if you walk all over me!'

'Don't shout at me!' she shouted, on a loud, anguished sob. 'I need to tell you something and it is hard for me!'

'Tell me what?' He was not going to make it easy for her. 'That you treat me like a football for my own good?'

'I was pregnant with your baby when you left me to go to your *papa*'s funeral!'

CHAPTER TEN

THE agonising confession left her lips at the same moment that the weather front moved in. Anton just froze where he stood as the sky blackened around him. Nothing moved on his face—nothing!

Christina was suffering from the opposite. She was shaking all over, her arms wrapping tightly around her body as if they were trying to hold it all in.

And she could not look at him. It hurt to look at him. As the first flash of lightning lit the room Luis spoke. 'Pregnant?' he repeated hoarsely. 'You were pregnant with our child and you didn't tell me?'

'I did not know then.' Staring fiercely at her bare feet, Cristina was fighting to hold back the tears now. 'I f-found out later—af-after you'd gone…'

It had all been so wonderfully perfect to her. She was in love with Luis and carrying his baby, and he was going to come back for her as soon as he could, and then they would—

'I wanted so much to tell you each time you called me on the telephone. But you were grieving for your *papa* and busy trying to walk in his shoes, so I decided to wait until you came back to Rio. But…'

The baby had not waited that long.

'I l-lost it, Before you came back for me…'

'How did you lose it?' he questioned huskily.

'I was working in the café when I got this—pain. The next thing I knew I was rushing to hospital in an ambulance. I was frightened and you were not there—'

154

Like a man who did not want anyone to see his expression, Anton spun his back to her, eyes closing as he listened to her trembling voice.

'I was in danger, they told me. The baby was not growing in the right place. And they said—they said that if they did not remove it I would—'

She stopped to swallow. It was too much. Anton spun round and attempted to take her in his arms. But Cristina didn't want that. She wanted—needed—to stand alone with this, because that was how she had dealt with it then. And it had all been so quick. One minute she was carrying Luis's beautiful baby, the next thing she knew she was—

She shrugged his hands away. 'W-when I woke up it was over,' she continued. 'They said there had been—complications. They had to remove—too much. There would be no more babies…'

'Dear God…' She heard him swallow.

'My—father arrived at my bedside.' Still she kept her eyes fixed on her bare feet. 'S-someone had contacted him when I w-was admitted. He…'

Stood over her like an angel of darkness and poured his shame and contempt over her. Accused her of sullying the Marques name.

'He w-wanted to know what use I was to him now that there would never be a grandson to inherit Santa Rosa. He…' She stopped to moisten her dry, trembling lips. 'He asked what kind of man would want to marry a barren woman.'

'Dear God,' Anton breathed. 'What kind of man was *he*, to say such a thing to you?'

'A desperate one,' Cristina answered. 'Santa Rosa was deep in debt even then. His only chance of saving it was to marry me off to some man willing to pay him well for the honour. I ran away when he first began parading his suitable candidates in front of me. That's when I met you, lived with you, became pregnant by you, and…'

She left the rest unsaid. Luis was Brazilian enough to know how things worked in the archaic corners of society. A nice young, protected virgin would win a high price on the marriage market. A spoiled one would earn much less.

A barren one was worth nothing.

The next crack of lightning lit the bedroom. Cristina folded her arms more tightly across her chest. 'The next time he came to the hospital he brought Vaasco with him,' she continued. 'Vaasco was willing to put a large injection of cash into Santa Rosa if I married him.'

'So you said yes, just like that?'

'No, I did not!' For the first time she lifted her eyes to him. He looked pale in the darkness of the room, shocked, appalled—revolted by her now? She looked away again. 'I s-sent them away,' she continued quietly. 'I n-needed time to be on my own, to grieve and to think. I had nowhere else to go so I returned to your apartment. There was a message from you waiting for me on the answering machine, telling me you were on your way to Rio. So I w-waited for you to come…' One of her hands unclipped itself from her arm and lifted to rub her trembling mouth before it dropped back down again. 'I was going to tell you what had happened, but we had that big row—'

'You needed to hurt me as you were hurting.'

'You were talking about marriage and babies.' Her voice choked on the memory. 'How do you think that made me feel, Luis? I was in love with you and I was hurting. I was in shock. Would you have preferred it if I had said yes to your marriage proposal and then said—By the way, Luis, there will be no children because I am barren, you see?'

'Yes, I would have preferred it,' he replied. 'I had a right to know. Do you think I would have walked away from you if you'd told me the truth?'

'I did not want to give you that choice.'

She heard his breath hiss from between his teeth. 'You blamed me.'

Cristina stared down at her feet and thought about it. Yes, she concluded, she had blamed him—for not being there when she needed him—but as for the rest…

Luis let out a sigh and moved right away from her. 'It's okay. Don't worry about it,' he muttered heavily. 'Right now I am blaming myself.'

'No.' Her head came up. 'I did not tell you this to make you feel guilty about it!'

'Then why did you tell me?'

'To make you see why I cannot marry you!'

'You married Ordoniz knowing you could not give him children. Why not me?' he bit out roughly.

'I did not care about him. I care about you.'

Anton pulled in an unsteady breath. 'The man was childless, Cristina,' he delivered painfully. 'Surely he must have married you so that you could give him a son?'

'I am not that wicked!' For the first time since this little scene had begun she let her eyes make contact with his. 'Why do you always have to look for the bad in me?'

She was right; he did. Hell, I'm losing my head here, Anton thought. And he wanted to—

'Vaasco could not have children!' she threw at him. 'He could not have sex! He—the accident,' she added on a shivering breath, 'the horse—it damaged him there. And he did *not* want me because I was young and for everything else I see twisting around in your head!' she threw at him. 'He wanted to punish me because I—I caused his accident, and…' She paused before asking warily, 'Has your mother explained what Vaasco was to her?'

'Oh, yes.' His mother had been totally honest with him—at last.

'Vaasco never forgave her,' Cristina said, then released a sudden cold laugh. 'He forgave Enrique Ramirez for his part in your *mamma*'s affair because he was a man, and ''a man is allowed to sip the nectar if it is there to sip''— Vaasco's words exactly,' she explained. 'He also knew about you and me—my father had told him. He expected you to come back for me. He wanted to watch me hurt you when you did. He wanted you to be hurt in your *mamma*'s place, by seeing me married to him. He made me stay in Rio with him for a full year, w-waiting for you to come back.'

But he hadn't come back.

'You let him do this to you without putting up a fight?'

Her eyes were cold now. 'He bought me from my father in the same way that you have been trying to buy me. When you sell yourself you lose the right to think for yourself.'

Anton turned away from that coldly honest statement, a hand with decidedly shaky fingers going up to scrape through his hair, then ending up grabbing the back of his neck.

What now? he asked himself as he stood there trying to numb the shockwaves crashing into him. Cristina was right about him. He did always look for the bad in her. He had done it six years ago, when he had taken what she'd said to him without bothering to question why she was saying it. What kind of man did that make him?

He had even come back here to Brazil bent on seeking his revenge on her for what she'd done. He need not have bothered. Cristina had been punishing herself.

He found he was staring at the bed, with its humble picnic, and suddenly he felt the sting of tears attack the back of his throat as he began to see every single thing she had done since he came back into her life for what it really was.

An act of love for him that was so damn hopeless in her eyes she had to be tough afterwards—or how did she let him go?

He turned to look at Cristina next, standing there in his T-shirt and his bowtie and nothing else. His scent on her body, his kisses on her lips. His love was wrapped all around her if she would dare to let herself to feel it.

'Let's go back to bed,' he said.

She stared at him. 'Have you listened to anything I have said to you?'

'All of it.' He nodded. 'It doesn't change a single thing.'

'Oh, *meu Dues*,' she sighed, as it all flared up again. 'Luis, I know about Enrique's last will and testament!' she cried. 'I know why you need to marry quickly and produce a child! You have half-brothers you need to—'

'Don't talk about them,' he uttered. They did not belong here—not in this room with this situation and this woman who had sacrificed so much! Well, he was about to learn what it felt like to sacrifice something he wanted badly. Because from this moment on he had no half-brothers. How could he have when—?

God, he did not want to go there right now. He could not allow himself to if he was going to get through the rest of this.

'We have to talk about them,' Cristina insisted. 'The only way you can meet them is by marrying s-some woman who can give you a baby…'

Anton stiffened. She didn't know—not all of it anyway.

'Well, you cannot do that with me,' she went on. 'S-so you can go now and—and marry that h-horrible Kinsella Lane person,' she suggested with tremulous bite.

He laughed. It was bad of him to laugh with so much

anguish creasing the atmosphere, but that was what he did. Because here stood this beautiful, proud, *tragic* woman telling him to go—yet she was protecting that damn door as if her life depended on it!

He heeled his shoes off. For a moment he thought she was going to leap on him in a rage. 'Luis—!'

'That's me,' he acknowledged, and pulled his shirt off over his head.

She stamped a foot. Now, that's more like it, he thought as he began to undo his trousers.

'If you don't stop this I will—!'

He reached her so fast that it was all she could do to gasp out a protest as he clamped his hand over her mouth. 'Now, listen to me…' he said, bringing his head down so he could look right into those dark pools of tragedy. 'I am *not* going to stop loving you because you think that I should, and I am *not* going to walk away from this. I *am* going to marry you, whether you like it or not, and I *am* going to keep on loving you until I draw my last breath— so get used to it.'

After that he straightened up, took his hand from her mouth and lowered it to grasp both her arms, where they still linked defensively across her front. He used them to pull her over to the bed. It took him five seconds to get rid of the tray, another two to grab her again, then stretch out on the bed, pulling her down on top of him so she had no option but to unwrap her arms to support herself.

Her eyes were dark and her mouth small, and as he looked up at her he knew she had not given in to him yet.

'Sad little thing,' he murmured, and stroked a gentle finger across an unhappy cheek. 'Am I such a bad bet?'

She gave a sombre shake of her head, *'Arido,'* she whispered.

It came then. Six years of grief and misery pouring out of her as she lowered her face to his chest and wept.

Anton said no more. He did not attempt to stem the flow. He just held her. Held her and wished there was something he could do to make it all go away for her—but there wasn't.

Arido, he thought bleakly, and rolled with her, pulled the covers up over them, then curled his body around her as much as he could.

Of course he ended up kissing her out of it. How long was a man supposed to lie passive while the woman in his arms broke her heart all over him?

And he used words—husky, soft, honest words—like, *'Eu te amo.'* I love you. *'Nada matérias outras.'* Nothing else matters. *'Eu te amo. Eu te amo.'* Until words became warm, thick, tear-washed kisses, and kisses became—something else. It even shocked him how an overdose of heartache and anguish could generate the driving depths of passion they ended up sharing.

Anton still wasn't over it when he carefully slid from beneath her and stood up from the bed. She was asleep, coiled around the pillow he'd slipped into the place where his body had been. Turning away, he hunted down his discarded clothes and put them on again with a dry promise that this time they'd stay on. Then he let himself out of the room as quietly as he could do.

He needed some time alone to think.

Cristina came awake to find she was hugging the pillow. She sat up, blinking owlishly, trying to decide if the grey light she could see seeping into the room was the fading day or a new day just come.

She felt hot and sweaty, and every one of her muscles ached as if she hadn't moved them for hours and hours.

She had a cloudy recollection of the events that had led up to her falling into a deep sleep here in this bed, but in truth she did not want to think about them.

Luis's bag still sat on the ottoman, but a swift glance around the room told her that he was not here. She got up, discovered she was wearing his T-shirt again—though she did not recall when she'd pulled it back on after—

She sucked in a sharp breath, not wanting to go there—not yet anyway. Instead she crossed the room to look out of the window, then bit out a very unladylike curse.

It *was* daylight out there! She had slept the evening and the whole of the night away—plus most of the morning too!

Spinning around, she headed quickly for her own bedroom, where she showered and pulled on clean jeans and a fresh green T-shirt, then tried to soothe her fidgety nerves before she went to find Luis. Only to receive the shock of her life when she found a man—a complete stranger—dressed in a suit, wandering the hall with a clipboard.

'Good morning, *senhorita*,' he greeted her politely when he saw her standing there on the stairs, then just continued with what he was doing!

Anger began to fizz. 'Do you happen to know where Senhor Scott-Lee is?' she demanded.

'I think most of them are in the kitchen,' he replied absently as he wandered off into one of the reception rooms.

Most of them?

Cristina headed for the kitchen. On her way there she passed one of the women from the village, coming away from the kitchen carrying a mop and bucket. She dipped a shy hello at Cristina and, when asked what she was doing, said she was here to help Orraca with the household chores.

Since Cristina did most of those chores herself, she took the fact that someone had given this woman a mop and bucket and told her to go and clean something as a very personal slight.

Luis, of course. It just had to be him. She'd given in to a little weak weeping on his shoulder and now he thought he could—

Those thoughts ground to a stop at the sight that met her in the kitchen. For a few seconds she could not believe what she was seeing, and even thought of going out and coming in again. For there at her table sat Orraca, sharing what looked like a pot of tea served in the best china with none other than Luis's mother, who was looking lovely in a soft cambric shirt and pale blue linen trousers, her dark hair loosely looped at her slender nape.

'Ah, good morning, Cristina,' the lady herself greeted her warmly.

'Good—morning.' Good manners made her reply accordingly.

Mrs Scott-Lee smiled. 'I can see you are surprised to see me here, and I don't blame you,' she said. 'When my son wishes to move mountains, he moves mountains. Please— come and sit down and join us. Orraca and I were just reminiscing about the old times.'

'How—how long have you been here?'

'I arrived just half an hour ago. But Anton's team of experts were here at the crack of dawn.'

'Team—?'

'The men who are surveying the land edging the forest with the intention of acquiring a protection order for it.'

'Protection?' She was bewildered.

'*Sim.* Anton thinks it is best to do it officially, then you will not have to put up with greedy people like the Alagoas Consortium coming at you through the back door, so to speak. Come and sit down,' his *mamma* urged yet again.

'Orraca, another cup and saucer, if you would be so good, my dear...'

Orraca, Cristina saw to her utter amazement, meekly stood from the table and did as she was bade—when no one, but *no one*, told Orraca to do anything!

Cristina's eyes gave a flash. 'Where is Luis?' she demanded.

'In Sao Paulo, dealing with some other business. He said to tell you to eat a proper breakfast before you start shouting at me,' his mother relayed, dark eyes twinkling, and so thoroughly, unfairly disarming that Cristina found herself sitting down and accepting the cup of tea Orraca provided, along with one of her unreadable stares.

'I suppose you think it is okay to let strangers wander my home?' she said to the housekeeper.

'He is an architect.' Mrs Scott-Lee provided the reply. 'An expert in historical renovation. And he is so in love with your house, Cristina, he almost begged Anton to give him the commission. What do you usually eat for breakfast, *meu querida*?'

'She does not eat breakfast.' Orraca spoke for the first time. 'She does not eat lunch. Why do you think she is so thin? I am amazed your handsome son wants to marry such a—'

'I think we will have some hot toast with proper butter,' Luis's mother smoothly cut in. 'I usually deny myself butter,' she confided. 'Not good for the figure or the heart. But, since you make your own here, how am I supposed to resist it?'

Orraca moved off without another word to make the suggested toast, while Cristina tried a couple of calming breaths before she attempted to make sense of what was going on here.

'Senhora Scott-Lee—'

'Please call me Maria—everyone does—except for Anton, of course. If you prefer it you can call me Mother, as he does, though I always think it's such a stuffy name—very English.' She grimaced.

'He is English,' Cristina said.

'You think so?' His mother looked thoughtful. 'I suppose he must seem it to you.'

'Mrs—Maria…'

'Still, you haven't met his uncle Maximilian yet. Now, there is the quintessential Englishman—complete with bowler hat and umbrella in his prime. Now he prefers Harris tweed and a walking stick.'

'*Senhora*—'

'Ah, here is our toast. Orraca, I think I would like to steal you away from Santa Rosa. Would you like to live in London, do you think?'

As it began to dawn on Cristina that she was not going to be allowed to ask any questions as to what was going on here, she took a piece of toast, liberally spread with butter, bit into it, and sipped her tea while the other two women slipped into conversation about the advantages and disadvantages of living abroad. She silently seethed.

She was going to kill Luis when he put in an appearance. Who did he think he was? Taking over her home as if he owned it just because she had agreed to—

She stood up. It was the shock that made her do it.

But she had said it—hadn't she? She had lain in his arms and said *yes* to his marriage proposal—his proper marriage proposal, complete with—

'Cristina, what's wrong?' his mother asked sharply.

'I want to see Luis,' she insisted tautly. 'I demand to see Luis!'

'*Querida*, he isn't here…'

'I am not your darling, Mrs Scott-Lee,' Cristina replied.

'I am *viuva de* Ordoniz—the woman you travelled thousands of miles to stop from marrying your son!'

'That was yesterday.' Maria touched Cristina's hand in a gentle conciliatory gesture. 'Today I could not be happier for both of you—'

'Why should you be?' Cristina demanded.

'Ah, here are my two handsome young escorts.' She smiled with relief as Luis's two executives appeared at the kitchen door. 'I hope this means that Anton has returned?' she enquired hopefully.

'He went straight to the library—'

'*My* library?' Cristina swung on them.

'Er—yes.' They were startled. She did not blame them. If Luis had been there to see her face he would be taking a very wary step back by now.

'Please excuse me,' she said, with an icy politeness that did not reflect what she was feeling inside.

Polite? she thought as she walked out of the kitchen, having to sidle past the woman from the village who was mopping the hall floor. Then she caught sight of the architect person, carefully scraping at the plaster on the walls. It was like being invaded, she thought as she stalked past him across the hall and pushed open the library door. Luis was there, all right, standing by *her* desk, using *her* telephone, dressed in a sharp dark pinstripe suit and giving off the arrogant appearance that he ruled the world!

Her world.

Cristina slammed the door shut to get his attention. He swung around and snatched her breath away, because he looked so big and lean and alive and—

'What do you think you are playing at?' she scythed at him.

The smile that had been about to arrive on his lips disappeared before it made it. With smooth aplomb Anton concluded his call and replaced the receiver on its rest. Then he settled his hips against the desk and just looked at her while he decided how he was going to tackle this.

The tempting way was to provoke what he could already see was erupting. The safer way was to soothe the situation down.

He went for the irresistible. 'You've forgotten.'

'Forgotten what?'

'That in a week you and I will be getting married,' he provided. 'It is usual to—'

'*A week?* I didn't think it would be so soon!'

'I moved the date up. I told you I was going to do it last night, when we—'

'All right.' She held up a hand. 'We will begin this stupid conversation again!' She took in a deep, calming breath. 'Luis—there is a man wandering around *my* house, picking plaster off the walls.'

'An architect.' He nodded.

'I know what he is!' she snapped. 'Your mother kindly informed me of it. I want to know when it was exactly that I gave my permission for him to be here!'

'You didn't. I did.'

'And your permission came from where?'

He sent her one of those seductively appealing lazy grins. 'I'm not answering that. I daren't,' he confided.

She frowned and crossed her arms. 'I believe there is also a team of surveyors on my property?'

He nodded in confirmation. 'After we marry. Santa Rosa will be placed in a trust—or have you forgotten about that too?'

'A trust for whom?' she almost choked out.

'Whoever you decide will inherit it from you.' He shrugged. 'Since we won't be able to spend all our time here it seemed sensible to protect Santa Rosa as much as is possible. The surveyors will also be looking at the forest. The Government frowns on deforestation these days. In fact I am amazed a protection order was not placed on it years ago.'

There was so much sense in what he was saying that he could see she was struggling to find an argument—though she did find one.

'I would have liked to be consulted about all of this *before* Santa Rosa was invaded.'

'No time,' he said. 'You were asleep and I needed to get things moving. My mother—'

'*Why* is your mother here?'

'She's not welcome?'

'Of course she's welcome.' Cristina frowned. 'But I—'

'She wants to help you choose your wedding outfit. But if you would rather she—'

'Luis—I am not marrying you!'

'Not that again.' He sighed. 'Which door would you like me to try and leave by, so you can have a running start at barring my way?'

She flushed. And so she should, Anton thought, losing enthusiasm for the provoking game. He had known she would change her mind again the moment she opened her eyes this morning. He had known that the tragic creature he'd loved in every way he could last night had only been recharging her batteries before she went on the defensive again. He'd meant to stay out of her way—had planned to do that right up until the moment he'd stood over her this morning, watching her sleep with his pillow clutched in her arms, and something had hit him.

The sense of honour that Sebastian must have instilled in him—because he sure as hell hadn't got it from his real father. Cristina deserved to have her say, even if it did mean yet another battle.

'I'm going to tell you something I had vowed to keep to myself. But having you continually try to make me walk away from you, I've changed my mind.'

Her chin came up in defensive readiness. Anton thought about going over there and just kissing her into surrender, then grimly stuck to his guns and pushed himself into speech.

'When Ramirez tempted me out to Brazil to look for you he did it with just one clever sentence that insisted I ''make reparation'' to the woman I ran out on six years before, leaving her in dire straits.'

'But you didn't do that.'

'Did I not?' He looked grimly at her whitened face. 'I thought I hadn't. I thought that you should be making rep- aration to me for the way you kicked me out of your life— but look at you, Cristina.' He indicated brutally. 'Look at the prickly, self-defensive, half-empty shadow you've be- come of that wonderful, excitingly vital and light-hearted creature I knew six years ago.'

She went pale. Anton sighed. 'Would you have become this person if I'd stayed around and fought for what I wanted? No, you would not,' he declared without expecting a reply. 'You would not have let your father sell you to some no-good vengeful swine because you didn't care what happened to you. You would have been mine! And, on being mine, you would have been pulled by your beautiful hair out of your shock and your grief and made to see that you did not need to be anything other than the beautiful person you are—to be loved by me! However, I walked,' he breathed in contempt. 'Which makes the accusation Ramirez made against me true. Because I *do* owe you— for not being man enough to stop still long enough to think *why* you needed to lash out at me. I owe you, *querida*, for six long miserable years of existing in a vacuum breaking your poor heart over me!'

She walked out. Anton stood there staring at the door she'd shut behind her. His hand went up to wipe the angry pallor from his face. He didn't know why she had walked out, or what she was thinking. He didn't even know if he'd just made the biggest mistake by telling her that he had his own guilt to feed.

CHAPTER ELEVEN

ORRACA found Cristina in her bedroom, staring out through the window.

'Enrique Ramirez is the English gaucho's *papa*. His *mamma* has just told me,' she announced. 'Enrique is the man who saved your life when I foolishly let go of your hand. He pulled that horse away from you at great risk to himself, never mind that swine Ordoniz. If Ramirez wants you to marry his son, then do it. You owe him that.'

'Everyone seems to owe everyone something,' Cristina murmured.

'*Sim,*' Orraca agreed. 'But a debt only becomes a burden if you do not want to pay it. You want to pay the debt, child, but you are too surrounded here by bad ghosts that tell you to turn the debt into a burden. Get away from here, Cristina,' the old woman advised. 'Marry the son of Enrique Ramirez, spit in the eye of the bad spirits and see what life brings.'

'Happiness?' She turned a sad smile on this woman who had been in her life for as long as Cristina could recall.

'If he is man enough to pull you free from this place, like his *papa* pulled that horse free, then he is man enough to give you happiness.'

Maybe Orraca was right. Maybe it was time to stop communing with ghosts—time to stop pulling against Luis.

'His *mama* is waiting downstairs to take you to Sao Paulo,' Orraca said. 'Go with her, buy the prettiest wedding outfit you can find, and marry your English gaucho. If he

171

turns out to be no good you can always come back here and be miserable again.'

Cristina laughed. She couldn't help it at such sober advice. Orraca just shrugged and left the room again.

Fifteen minutes later, Cristina was sitting beside her future mother in law in a helicopter, flying to Sao Paulo.

Anton watched them go from one of the windows. She would not be coming back here before they married—though Cristina didn't know that yet, he reminded himself. Nor would she be seeing him again until they stood in front of the registrar and made their vows—if his mother got Cristina that far, that was.

He turned away from the window, a wry smile playing with the corners of his mouth. His mother was the best gentle bully he knew, but could she handle Cristina if she took fright again and decided to make a run for it?

He had Santa Rosa covered as a place to escape to, because he was staying right here until the morning they married in Rio. And Gabriel Valentim no longer held a reliable bolt-hole because the man was too much the romantic. Gabriel was so convinced that Cristina belonged with Anton that he had agreed to be his best man. And even Rodrigo Valentim had been convinced that he had Cristina's best interests at heart.

The lawyer had listened to everything Anton had said to him this morning in Sao Paulo, and carefully read the documents he'd placed in front of him which showed that if Cristina could not be happy in their marriage then Santa Rosa would always be here for her, safe and cared for by the trust he was setting up to protect it. Then he'd played his ace card and asked Rodrigo if he would give the bride away. Recalling the way the older man had filled up, Anton was prepared to trust that Rodrigo Valentim's home would not be a safe bolt-hole for Cristina to use either.

If all of those people managed to get Cristina to stand in front of the registrar, then it only left him with the prospect of a full blown face-to-face rejection in front of everyone in the Blue Room at his hotel in Rio.

Could he handle that?

Yes, he could handle it. He could handle anything—because this time he was not going to let Cristina down. And on that final thought, he turned his attention to the next grim task in hand.

Going to sit down behind the desk of the late Lorenco Marques, Luis put his mind into a different gear, then picked up the phone.

Two minutes later a cool, smooth, quietly refined voice greeted him pleasantly. 'Good afternoon, Senhor Scott-Lee. It is a pleasure to hear from you.'

'It's quite possible that you won't be saying that in a few seconds, Senhor Estes,' Anton replied. 'I am calling you to formally withdraw any claim I have on Enrique Ramirez's estate.'

There was a small silence. 'May I enquire as to why you've made this decision?'

'That's personal.'

'Your half-brothers—'

'Will survive without knowing me.'

'But will you survive without knowing them, *senhor*?'

The quick answer? Anton mused. 'Yes.' If he had to.

'You do understand that by doing this your share of your father's estate—'

'Ramirez was not my father.'

'A moot point we will leave to one side for now, if you will. As I was saying…You understand that your share in the estate will go to Cristina Marques?'

'Since you've already handed over a chunk of it to her

I think I've managed to get that, Senhor Estes,' Anton drawled. 'Was that ethical, by the way?'

'Was it ethical that you brought your mistress with you to Rio?' the lawyer returned.

Anton sat up straight. 'Explain that,' he commanded.

'I think you prefer to call her your secretary,' Senhor Estes said.

'So the money went to Cristina as a slap on the wrist for me? Is that what you mean?'

'Your—Enrique Ramirez expected you to mend your lusty ways not continue them.'

'I don't bed two women at the same time, Senhor Estes,' Anton said coldly. 'Unlike my—father, who seems to have bedded anything he happened to see in a skirt.'

'He was not the most discerning of men where his personal life was concerned,' the lawyer agreed. 'May I ask why you will not be marrying Cristina Marques?

'But I am marrying Cristina,' Anton confirmed smoothly. 'On Saint Sebastian's day at two p.m. in the Blue Room at my hotel. You are welcome to attend, if you wish.'

'I will certainly consider it,' the other man said politely. 'Though I don't see the point if you are definitely pulling out of this.'

'I am.' Anton was adamant.

'Then you will understand that from that day forth all correspondence to do with Enrique Ramirez's estate will be forwarded to your wife?'

'Of course,' Anton agreed. 'Prefixed by my name, if you please, Senhor Estes, since I will be taking complete control of Cristina's business interests from that day forth.'

There was a pause, a long pause, then the merest hint of smile sounded in Senhor Estes's tone. 'Machismo still rules on the pampas, heh, Mr Scott-Lee?'

'Most certainly,' Anton confirmed.

'Then all correspondence from this office to your wife will be prefixed by your name,' the lawyer established.

'And, as I will be attending all meetings with or on behalf of my wife, may I ask if she will need to attend any meetings at your offices with regard to Enrique's estate?'

'That will of course, be up to your wife.'

'Thank you.'

'Please don't mention it,' the other man said, and there was a definite smile in his voice now. 'Before you go, Mr Scott-Lee, I am curious—do you know why your father took so personal an interest in Miss Marques?'

Anton tensed. 'I believe he saved her life once.'

'And a life once saved becomes the saviour's responsibility,' the lawyer confirmed. 'Enrique lived by that maxim where Cristina was concerned. He even found her a job working in a café-bar on the Copacabana when she ran away from home seven years ago—though I don't think that she knows this. It was purely coincidental, of course, that the café-bar was the place you used to frequent each evening on your way home from the bank. Fate lending a hand, do you think, Mr Scott-Lee?'

It did not take Anton two seconds to understand what Estes was really saying. Anger erupted, pushing him to his feet. 'Then where the hell was Ramirez when Cristina needed protecting from her father and that bastard Ordoniz?' he rasped.

'Enduring his first heart attack,' the lawyer came back. 'Where were you, Senhor Scott-Lee...?'

Anton was pacing. He had never thought he would be a pacer at his own wedding. He'd always teased his friends when they'd done this at their weddings. Now here he was—pacing.

She was late.

He glanced at his watch. Not very late, just a few minutes late—the bride's prerogative.

'Anton…' Gabriel touched him on the shoulder.

He swung round. One glance at the other man's face and he knew his worst prediction was about to come true.

'Where is she?' he demanded.

'Not far,' Gabriel quickly assured him. 'She's at the restaurant downstairs, by the pool. She wants to talk to you before she—'

The rest was spoken into fresh air.

Anton stepped outside and saw her instantly. She was sitting at a table staring at the ornamental pool—and he had to pause for a moment because she quite simply took his breath away. Her hair was down, rippling in glossy, loose spiral twists down her back, and she was wearing a simple short silk sheath dress in a shade of warm ocean-green that could have been hand-dyed to match the colour of his eyes.

Relief swept through him. A woman who bought a dress to match the colour of her lover's eyes had not been thinking of jilting him when she chose it. As he approached he even smiled when he caught sight of what she was wearing to tie her hair back from her face.

'Hi,' he said as he arrived beside her, touching her warm sun-kissed shoulder with his fingertips and bending to brush a kiss to her cheek.

'Hi,' she greeted him huskily.

Swinging out the chair next to hers, he turned it around, then straddled it.

Cristina glanced up and felt not just her heart but everything else take a warm, swooping dive inside her. He looked so very good to her hungry eyes, with his neat dark hair and warm golden skin, and a smile on his lips that made her vulnerable heart ache. He was wearing a pale cream silk-linen suit that did disturbing things for his broad-shouldered figure, and the silk shirt he wore beneath the jacket was an almost exact match to the colour of her dress.

'Now I know why my mother bought this shirt and insisted I wear it,' he said. Reaching out then, he flicked a finger at the cream ribbon she was wearing in her hair. 'And you've been filching my bow ties again.'

Cristina flushed and looked away. 'Don't tease,' she shook out.

A waiter appeared beside their table. Without hesitation Luis ordered two glasses of champagne. The waiter moved away—curious, Cristina could tell, because it had to be obvious that they were the bride and groom supposed to be getting married in the Blue Room right now, instead of sitting here. Luis was even wearing a creamy rosebud in his jacket lapel.

'Luis…' she whispered anxiously.

'Mmm?' he responded, in an intimately seductive way that brought some colour into her pale cheeks.

Leaning forward, he rested his arms across the back of the chair, then placed his chin on his arms. 'You look amazingly, beddably gorgeous, *meu querida*,' he told her softly. 'Will you come upstairs and marry me?'

Cristina sucked in a breath. 'Can you be serious for a moment?'

'Not today, no,' he refused.

'But I need to talk to you—'

'You could try looking at me when you say that, my darling. At the moment you are talking to your poor mangled fingers.'

Her chin shot up; her eyes flashed. 'Will you please listen to me for one moment without—'

'Listen to you try to kick me out of your life again? No way.' Anton shook his head.

'I don't want—'

'Then what do you want?' he asked, and the humour was starting to leave him, no matter what he'd said about refusing to be serious.

'I want to talk about what you really want,' she told him.

'I want you as my wife.'

The champagne arrived, delivered to the table with a flourish in two fluted glasses. 'With the compliments of the hotel, *senhor—senhora.*' The waiter smiled, then melted away.

'He thinks we are already married.' Cristina sighed.

'Optimistic of him—but then he doesn't know my bride's penchant for pulling my strings.'

'You're cross.'

'Getting there,' Anton agreed as he handed her a glass. 'Now, drink,' he commanded. 'You are going to need Dutch courage to sustain you when I become weary of this and decide to pick you up and throw you over my shoulder—and don't kid yourself I won't do it,' he added warningly. 'Because you know very well that I will.'

'This just isn't fair! If you had agreed to speak to me on the telephone we would not be sitting here at all!'

A sleek black eyebrow made a sardonic arch. 'You wanted to dump me by telephone this time?'

'I'm going to hit you in a minute.' She glared at him.

'Well, that would be a whole lot healthier than sitting here giving the impression that you are about to attend a wake,' Anton snapped, then uttered a sigh. 'You know that I love you, Cristina,' he declared wearily. 'I've tried to show you I do in every which way I can. But if you cannot find it in you to love me enough to want to spend the rest of your life with me, then I *will* accept that and let you go.'

'I don't feel like that.' Cristina even shivered at the thought of him letting her go. But her eyes were bleak as they stared into her champagne glass. 'You are being asked to sacrifice too much for me, Luis.'

'We aren't talking about me, now. We are talking about you and what you want.'

'I want more than anything for you to be happy.'

'And you believe that you are the best one to judge what will make me happy?' His tone alone mocked her ability to judge anything with any accuracy.

'Your half-brothers,' she said huskily. 'I cannot let you sacrifice the chance of meeting them because I cannot—'

'They are not an issue,' he interrupted. 'Seriously,' he added, at her impatient look, 'they are not an issue. You are the issue, Cristina. You know it and I know it, so get to the point.'

'I don't think that *I* can be truly happy again,' she admitted on a helpless rush. 'And that could make you unhappy—understand?'

'You could be right.' Anton was not going to pull his punches here, this was just too important, but he did reach out to gently move a stray twist of hair from her unhappy cheek. 'I know I can never fill that empty place you carry around inside you, and that does make me unhappy, but I would rather live with it than live without you.'

'And what about the empty place that you will carry around inside *you* because you can never conceive your own child with me?'

Anton heaved in a sigh and straightened his body. He spied his mother standing anxiously by, not far away, and knew she wanted to approach them, but he stopped her with a small frowning glance.

'I wish you had met Sebastian.' He turned back to Cristina. 'If you had met him you would know what a true father really is, and then you would not have needed to ask me that question. Sebastian was—special.'

'I know.' Cristina nodded. 'You used to talk a lot about him six years ago, w-when…'

'What you do not know is that Sebastian always knew that I was not his real son,' Anton told her, and watched her gaze flick to his in surprise. He held it there. 'Yet he loved me, Cristina, totally and unstintingly, from the moment I arrived in his world. My being someone else's son just did not matter to him. And if there is one thing I wish I could have changed in my relationship with him I wish I had known that he was not my blood father before he died, so I could have shown him how gut-wrenchingly *grateful* I feel for his loving me the way that he did.'

His voice had roughened with feeling—the same feeling that was showing on his face. Cristina wanted to reach out and soothe it away, but he had not finished.

'Well, I can do that,' he avowed. 'I can love someone else's child like that, because I had the best to show me how to do it. The point is, though, Cristina—can *you* do it? Can you take someone else's child into your life and allow it to fill that empty space inside you, as Sebastian allowed me to fill that empty place inside him?'

He was talking about adoption here. Filling their lives with other people's children and filling her with that dangerous thing called hope. Could she do it? Would it really be enough for him?

'But you *can* have your own child if you want to,' she persisted. 'It has to make a difference to how you feel! Maybe not now,' she conceded. 'But in years to come you might feel differently, and—'

'We don't live in the Dark Ages any more, when a man's only quest in life was to pass on his genes to the next generation,' he cut in. 'We've managed to evolve, look for other quests in life to chase—mine being getting a wedding ring on your finger, if you would only stop being so damn stubborn about this!'

'You really don't mind that we will have to adopt our children?'

'One, two, five—ten! Hell, Cristina, I don't care how many it takes to make you feel better about yourself! We could fill Santa Rosa with them if that's what you would like to do.'

'Or bring up a dozen little banker's children in England,' she added, with one of her impulsive little laughs.

The little laugh did it. Anton had had enough. That laugh told him he had her hooked, whether she wanted to be hooked or not. He stood up and swung the chair out of his way, then tugged his bride into his arms and kissed her—hard.

She fell into that kiss as she always did, without an ounce of control. By the time he pulled back she was wrapped to him, clinging and wanting more.

'Can we go and get married now?' he requested hopefully.

Cristina looked up at him, all dark, glowing eyes. 'I love you so much it frightens me,' she confided. 'But if you are absolutely sure this is what you want, Luis, then, yes.' She smiled. 'Let's go and get married.'

At last! Anton almost shouted it. Instead he contained the urge and drew her beneath his arm. As he turned them towards the restaurant exit his mother began to approach with one of her anxiously hopeful smiles. She received a kiss from her son, then one from her future daughter, and all three of them walked arm in arm back inside the hotel.

A very short half-hour later Anton turned to kiss his new wife. Then their small group of well-wishers crowded in and they were separated by everything but their clasped hands.

Cristina was flushed and happy. *He* was happy—and relieved that it was finally done.

Someone tapped him on the shoulder. He turned to find an immaculately dressed young man standing beside him—a young man Anton had seen before, right here in this hotel.

'My apologies for intruding, *senhor*,' the young man said. 'I have been instructed to pass this letter to you.'

The letter changed hands, then the young man bowed politely, turned, and walked out of the room.

Everyone else had gone silent. Anton smiled as he split the seal.

'What is it?' Cristina was suddenly at his elbow—clinging to it.

Without saying a word he handed her the envelope while he opened the single sheet of paper that had been inside. He could sense her puzzlement, her growing confusion.

'Looks good, hmm?' he prompted. 'Cristina Vitória de Marques Scott-Lee.'

'But it says care of you.' She frowned. 'I don't understand.'

Anton did. He handed her the letter. 'Wedding present,' he explained.

She read, then had to re-read what was written before it finally began to sink in. Then one of those pained little whimpers broke from her throat as she spun around.

'Rodrigo—' She held the letter out to her lawyer with trembling fingers. 'Please explain this to me!'

Rodrigo glanced at Anton, took the letter, glanced at it, then handed it back again. 'It's quite clear, *minha amiga*,' he said. 'On marrying Senhor Scott-Lee you became one of the three beneficiaries of the estate of the late Enrique

Ramirez. That makes you a very wealthy woman,' he added gravely.

'But how—why?' she demanded in complete bewilderment.

'By default,' the lawyer provided.

'I didn't want it,' Anton put in.

Cristina turned wide, horror-filled eyes on him. 'But, Luis, this belongs to you. *I* don't want it!'

'Don't say that,' he groaned. 'I've banked everything on you accepting it.'

Then he banded his arms around her so he could lift her off the ground and carry her away from the wedding group to a quiet corner of the room. Their faces were level—just how he liked it. He pressed small smiling kisses to her worried mouth as he walked.

'You are beautiful. I adore you. And you are going to be *such* a wealthy wife too.'

'Did you know this was going to happen?' she demanded, between the kisses.

'Of course.' He lowered her feet to the floor.

'Then why are you happy?'

'Because, *minha esposa bonita*, I get to have my cake and eat it.' He kissed her again.

'Talk sense to me!' Cristina snapped, prising their mouths apart.

'I never wanted Enrique's money, but I did want to meet my two half-brothers,' he informed her, more seriously.

'I still don't understand,' she sighed.

'It's simple—stop glaring at me. Enrique demanded certain—things from me before I could meet my half-brothers.'

'A wife and a baby,' she whispered bleakly.

'No, *querida*,' Anton said gently. 'He demanded I take *you* as my wife and *we* produce a baby—no, don't look sad again,' he chided. 'This is not a sad occasion, I promise you. Enrique was a cruel bastard, but I think he must have known that we would not be able to fulfil his demands. I hate having to do it, but I will even say that he planned things to conclude this way.'

Cristina crossed her arms. 'I wish I knew what this conclusion is that you keep walking circles around!'

'You and me finding each other, ending up here like this,' Anton explained. 'He wanted me to dance to his tune. He wanted me to fight tooth and nail to marry you, but he didn't want me to do that while still lying to myself that I was only marrying you to fulfil *his* wishes and not my own. And here is his cruelty, *cara*. He built a knockback into his plans to force me to face myself.' Anton grimaced. 'He didn't need to do that. I'd faced what I still felt for you within the first twenty-four hours of seeing you again.'

'The knockback was the baby I cannot give you.'

'I think he also knew that once I had met my half-brothers I would tell his lawyer where to put his money. So he made certain that I wouldn't have the option to refuse. Instead it would go to you, and I would be forced to take care of it.'

'I can take care of my own money.' Her chin came up.

Anton sent her a rueful smile. 'I hope not, Cristina. In fact I'm banking on you handing over full control of all your business interests to me.'

He took the letter from her and made her read the final paragraph.

You are invited to attend a meeting at the office of Estes and Associates at four p.m. on February fourteenth, to hear the final reading of the last will and testament of Enrique Ramirez, in the presence of the other main beneficiaries.

'Your half-brothers.'

'*If* they have jumped through the hoops I don't doubt Enrique set for them, as he did for me.'

'Your brothers…'

It was beginning to dawn on her. He could see the light beginning to glow in her eyes. 'You are going to attend the meeting in my place, because you are so full of machismo, so domineering and arrogant and…you love me for it, hmm?'

Cristina laughed. Anton laughed. The watching wedding group on the other side of the room gave a communal sigh of relief.

Champagne corks popped. The day moved on in a slow and easy romantic kind of way neither Anton or Cristina were in rush to bring to an end.

Eventually it did, though, and they went to their suite and to bed. Being officially man and wife added a delicious new level to their loving. Later, Anton was in his usual wide-awake relaxed sprawl while Cristina lay on top of him like a second skin.

'Valentine's Day,' he murmured thoughtfully.

'Mmm?' Cristina really did not want to raise herself out of the sated haze she was drifting in right now.

'February the fourteenth—Valentine's Day. I wonder who the die-hard romantic is that picked that particular date for me and my brothers to meet?'

'Your father?'

'Hmm, no.' He shook his head. 'I had several more months left to fulfil his wishes. I have to assume—*hope*— that having the date of the meeting brought forward like this means that, like me, my brothers must have hit their required targets earlier than expected.'

'You did not hit your target. You defaulted,' some imp made Cristina remind him.

'But I made sure I hooked in the woman who was going to get my share of the booty.' He smiled. 'I'm a winner—always have been.'

'And arrogant.'

'That too.'

'I can still remove my permission for you to attend that meeting in my place.'

'But you won't.'

'No.' She cuddled closer. 'I wonder if your brothers will look like you?' she pondered curiously. 'Can you imagine not one but *three* tall, dark, arrogant men strutting around as if they own the world?' She affected a shudder.

'We will probably hate each other on sight.'

Cristina lifted up her head and touched a gentle finger to his mouth. 'You are worried about meeting them?'

Anton tried for a macho indifferent shrug, but ended up sighing out a much more honest, 'Yes… And hellishly excited about it too. In fact—' he moved, using an arm to haul her further up his body '—too excited. I need a diversion.'

'Sex is going to be a diversion?'

'Making love to my beautiful demanding wife,' he corrected. 'The best diversion there is…'

Introducing a brand-new miniseries

FOR *Love* OR MONEY

This is romance on the red carpet...

For Love or Money is the ultimate reading experience
for the reader who has a taste for tales of wealth and
celebrity and the accompanying gossip and scandal!

Look out for the special covers
and
these upcoming titles:

Coming in November:
SALE OR RETURN BRIDE
by Sarah Morgan
#2500

Coming in December:
TAKEN BY THE HIGHEST BIDDER
by Jane Porter
#2508

Harlequin Presents®
The ultimate emotional experience!

HARLEQUIN® *Presents*

Seduction and Passion Guaranteed!

www.eHarlequin.com

HPSORB

Christmas comes to

HARLEQUIN ROMANCE®

In November 2005, don't miss:

MISTLETOE MARRIAGE
(#3869)

by Jessica Hart

For Sophie Beckwith, this Christmas means
facing the ex who dumped her and then married
her sister! Only one person can help: her best friend
Bram. Bram used to be engaged to Sophie's sister,
and now, determined to show the lovebirds that
they've moved on, he's come up with a plan: he's
proposed to Sophie!

Then in December look out for:

CHRISTMAS GIFT: A FAMILY
(#3873)

by Barbara Hannay

Happy with his life as a wealthy bachelor,
Hugh Strickland is stunned to discover he has
a daughter. He wants to bring Ivy home—but he's
absolutely terrified! Hugh hardly knows Jo Berry,
but he pleads with her to help him—surely the ideal
solution would be to give each other the perfect
Christmas gift: a family....

Available wherever Harlequin books are sold.

www.eHarlequin.com   HRXMAS

If you enjoyed what you just read,
then we've got an offer you can't resist!

Take 2 bestselling
love stories FREE!
Plus get a FREE surprise gift!

Clip this page and mail it to Harlequin Reader Service®

IN U.S.A.
3010 Walden Ave.
P.O. Box 1867
Buffalo, N.Y. 14240-1867

IN CANADA
P.O. Box 609
Fort Erie, Ontario
L2A 5X3

YES! Please send me 2 free Harlequin Presents® novels and my free surprise gift. After receiving them, if I don't wish to receive anymore, I can return the shipping statement marked cancel. If I don't cancel, I will receive 6 brand-new novels every month, before they're available in stores! In the U.S.A., bill me at the bargain price of $3.80 plus 25¢ shipping & handling per book and applicable sales tax, if any*. In Canada, bill me at the bargain price of $4.47 plus 25¢ shipping & handling per book and applicable taxes**. That's the complete price and a savings of at least 10% off the cover prices—what a great deal! I understand that accepting the 2 free books and gift places me under no obligation ever to buy any books. I can always return a shipment and cancel at any time. Even if I never buy another book from Harlequin, the 2 free books and gift are mine to keep forever.

106 HDN DZ7Y
306 HDN DZ7Z

Name	(PLEASE PRINT)	
Address	Apt.#	
City	State/Prov.	Zip/Postal Code

Not valid to current Harlequin Presents® subscribers.

Want to try two free books from another series?
Call 1-800-873-8635 or visit www.morefreebooks.com.

* Terms and prices subject to change without notice. Sales tax applicable in N.Y.
** Canadian residents will be charged applicable provincial taxes and GST.
All orders subject to approval. Offer limited to one per household.
® are registered trademarks owned and used by the trademark owner and or its licensee.

PRES04R   ©2004 Harlequin Enterprises Limited

eHARLEQUIN.com

The Ultimate Destination for Women's Fiction

Your favorite authors are just a click away
at www.eHarlequin.com!

- Take a sneak peek at the covers and
  read summaries of **Upcoming Books**

- Choose from over 600
  author **profiles!**

- Chat with your favorite authors
  on our **message boards.**

- Are you an author in the making?
  Get advice from published authors
  in **The Inside Scoop!**

**Learn about your favorite authors
in a fun, interactive setting—
visit www.eHarlequin.com today!**

INTAUTH04R

INTERNATIONAL
DOCTORS

They're guaranteed
to raise your pulse!

Meet the most eligible medical men of the world,
in a series of stories by popular authors that
will make your heart race!

Whether they're saving lives or dealing with desire,
our doctors have bedside manners that
send temperatures soaring....

Coming in November 2005:

THE ITALIAN DOCTOR'S MISTRESS
by *Catherine Spencer*
#2503

Pick up a Harlequin Presents® novel and you will enter a world
of spine-tingling passion and provocative, tantalizing romance!

Available wherever Harlequin books are sold.

HARLEQUIN®
Presents

Seduction and Passion Guaranteed!

www.eHarlequin.com

HPTIDM

Coming Next Month

HARLEQUIN *Presents*

THE BEST HAS JUST GOTTEN BETTER!